Frederic Lawrence Knowles

A Kipling Primer

Including Biographical and Critical Chapters, an Index to Mr. Kipling's ...

Frederic Lawrence Knowles

A Kipling Primer
Including Biographical and Critical Chapters, an Index to Mr. Kipling's ...

ISBN/EAN: 9783337010805

Printed in Europe, USA, Canada, Australia, Japan

Cover: Foto ©Raphael Reischuk / pixelio.de

More available books at **www.hansebooks.com**

A Kipling Primer

Including Biographical and Critical Chapters,
an Index to Mr. Kipling's Principal
Writings, and Bibliographies

By

FREDERIC LAWRENCE KNOWLES

Editor of
"Golden Treasury of American Lyrics," etc.

BOSTON
BROWN AND COMPANY
1899

𝕽𝖔𝖈𝖐𝖜𝖊𝖑𝖑 𝖆𝖓𝖉 𝕮𝖍𝖚𝖗𝖈𝖍𝖎𝖑𝖑 𝕻𝖗𝖊𝖘𝖘
BOSTON, U.S.A.

To My Father

Prefatory Note

THIS little book has been written in the hope that it may minister to an intelligent appreciation of Mr. Kipling's prose and poetry. The world has never before witnessed the spectacle of a collected edition of an author's works issued within a dozen years of the date on his earliest title-page. A body of criticism is bound to grow up around the writings of a genius so commanding and brilliant. If the *Primer* serve as an unpretentious forerunner of this literature, it asks nothing more.

In assigning stories and poems to their respective volumes, I have made reference not to the sumptuous and expensive *Outward Bound* edition, but to the Appleton editions of *The Seven Seas* and *Many Inventions*, Century Company editions of the *Jungle Books*, Doubleday & McClure editions of the *Day's Work* and *From Sea to Sea*, and Macmillan editions of the remaining books.

It should be said, however, that several of the early collections of stories are in a few instances contained in one volume. For example, Macmillan has bound together *Soldiers Three*, *The Story of the Gadsbys*, and *In Black and White* under the general title *Soldiers Three*. But a tale from *In Black and White* is in this *Primer* assigned to that book, not to *Soldiers Three*. The Macmillan edition of *Under the Deodars* contains also *The Phantom 'Rickshaw, and Other Tales* and *Wee Willie Winkie, and Other Stories*. The same rule has been observed in this volume as in the other.

In the *Outward Bound* edition the order of the tales is different, the contents having been rearranged by Mr. Kipling on a more logical plan. Of the two volumes devoted to the *Jungle Books*, for instance, the first contains all the tales in which Mowgli figures. It very properly concludes with " In the Rukh," transferred from *Many Inventions*. The second volume contains the stories in the *Jungle Books* which have no reference to Mowgli, such as " Quiquern," " The White Seal," and " Rikki-Tikki-Tavi." " Under *Soldiers Three* will be found all the events in which Mulvaney, Ortheris, and Learoyd were concerned, followed by other military stories. *In Black and White* covers tales of native life in India, and *The Phantom 'Rickshaw* those which deal with matters more or less between the two worlds." *Life's Handicap* and *Many Inventions* do not appear among the titles of the *Outward Bound* edition, the stories in those books being distributed among several volumes.

Appended to the abstracts of stories and ballads, in Chapter Three, will be found, in many cases, brief criticisms from well-known authorities. These are included for their suggestiveness rather than for any value as final estimates. Indeed, the editor has been at no pains to add them to all or even to most of the outlines, nor has he in any case endeavored to harmonize them with one another. While in the main they are astute, and doubtless trustworthy, in many instances they will be found chiefly to illustrate the fact that opinions even of high authorities are merely personal estimates and frequently prove to be very wide of the mark.

I wish to thank the assistants in the Boston Public and Harvard College libraries for numerous courtesies, and especially to thank Mr. Capen, Librarian of the Haverhill (Mass.) City Library, for his generous aid and coöperation.

TILTON, N.H., May 1, 1899.

SECOND NOTE.

As this book is on the point of going to press (July 1), there appears an inexpensive set of Mr. Kipling's works in fifteen volumes, authorized and copyrighted by the author. Except for the inclusion of *From Sea to Sea* in two volumes and the addition of *Departmental Ditties* to the volume containing *Barrack-Room Ballads*, the contents and arrangement of this edition call for no changes in the *Kipling Primer*. *Life's Handicap* and *Many Inven-*

tions are retained among the titles of this latest edition, and the author has in general followed the arrangement of the earlier volumes, on which this handbook is based, rather than the arrangement of the *Outward Bound* edition.

JULY 5, 1899.

Contents

CHAPTER III

A Kipling Primer

CHAPTER ONE

BIOGRAPHICAL SKETCH

1. BIRTH AND PARENTAGE. — Rudyard Kipling was born Dec. 30, 1865, in Bombay, India. His father's ancestors were English and Dutch; his mother's English, Scotch, and Irish. Both his grandfathers were Wesleyan ministers.

Rudyard's father, John Lockwood Kipling, was born in Yorkshire, and passed the early years of his manhood in the Burslem (Staffordshire) potteries as a modeller and designer. On leaving the potteries he worked for a time in a sculptor's studio, and finally received an appointment on the staff of the executive art department of the South Kensington Museum. In 1865 he was appointed Professor of Architectural Sculpture in the School of Art at Bombay. After having been engaged for several years in making casts of the mythological sculpture of the Rock Cut Temples in the central provinces,

he was appointed curator of the Government
Museum at Lahore. Mr. Kipling is said to have
done more than any other man toward preserving
the native art of India.

The poet's father was more, however, than a
mere artist, in the narrower sense. His scholarly
and literary aptitudes are shown in *Beast and Man
in India*, 1891, a book which brought him wide and
well-deserved recognition. Regarding his personality, Mr. E. Kay Robinson, who knew the family
intimately at Lahore, has this testimony : " John
Lockwood Kipling, the father, a rare, genial soul,
with happy artistic instincts, a polished literary style,
and a generous, cynical sense of humor, was, without exception, the most delightful companion I had
ever met." [1]

Rudyard's mother was a Miss Alice Macdonald,
daughter of the Methodist preacher at Endon, Staffordshire, and a young woman of great beauty. She
was one of three sisters who were noted for their
exceptional culture and talents. Both of the others
married distinguished English artists, one being the
wife of Sir Edward J. Poynter, president of the
Royal Academy, and the other the wife of Sir
Edward Burne-Jones. Mr. Robinson has written
also of Mrs. Kipling : " Mrs. Kipling, the mother,
preserved all the graces of youth, and had a sprightly,

---

[1] *McClure's Magazine*, July, 1896. See also Boston *Transcript*, March 2, 1899, and *Congregationalist*, March 16, 1899.

if occasionally caustic wit, which made her society always desirable." [1]

Such were the parents of the most eminent of living poets. He was born into an atmosphere of ideal charm and culture, and yet the circumstances of his birth in the great cosmopolitan city of western India left much to be desired. There is sincere pathos in those lines of *The Native-Born :*

> " We learned from our wistful mothers
> To call old England ' home.' "

2. CHILDHOOD. — Rudyard Kipling was named from Rudyard Lake, Staffordshire, on the banks of which John Kipling first met Miss Alice Macdonald. As a child the poet was familiarly called " Ruddie." It is interesting to learn that as he grew in years he "scorned all playthings that were commonplace toys; but any sort of instructive puzzle or game that required thought and intelligence appealed to him at once, and with these he found endless pleasure and pastime." When, under his mother's guidance, he had once mastered the art of reading, it was difficult to get him to play with the other boys. He was precocious, and filled with curiosity on all subjects.

The first five years of his life, excepting a short visit to England with his mother, were spent in his native city or its neighborhood, but in 1871 he was

---

[1] *McClure's*, July, 1896.

taken to England and left, together with a younger
sister, in the care of an elderly relative at Southsea.
Here, as it is generally believed, he spent several
unhappy years.   If it is true that *Baa, Baa, Black
Sheep* and the opening chapter of *The Light that
Failed* are largely autobiographical, we can only
wonder that Rudyard escaped growing up sullen
and embittered.   It must be admitted that he was
strong-willed and impetuous, and never an " easy
boy to manage," yet no amount of repressive and
ill-advised methods of discipline sufficed to take from
him his healthy outlook on life or enjoyment of its
pleasures.

Perhaps it was well, however, that he was not kept
longer in his uncongenial surroundings.   In 1877
his mother visited him, and his father joined her the
following year.   The boy spent several weeks with
the senior Kipling in Paris, and when his parents
returned to India, in 1878, he was entered as a
pupil at the United Service College of Westward
Ho, at Bideford, North Devon.

3. SCHOOLDAYS. — Westward Ho, thus named
from Charles Kingsley's story (it was within two
miles of Amyas Leigh's house at Northam), stood
on the shore of the British Channel.   It was under
the direction almost wholly of civil or military officers, and the pupils were chiefly officers' sons who
eventually went into the Indian service.   Rudyard
Kipling was noted at school principally for his wit,

his gift of story-telling, and his facility at writing. He held for two years the editorship of the *United Service College Chronicle*, where many bright verses and articles appeared over his signature. As a scholar he was not distinguished, though he was extraordinarily quick at any intellectual problem when he chose to apply his mind to it, and he carried away from the institution a well-deserved first prize in English literature. If one cares to know the schoolboy Kipling one must read the Stalky stories, where the nascent author figures as " Beetle." " Stalky " and " McTurk " were Beresford and Dunsterville, who shared Kipling's study and were his sworn confederates. Each one of the trio has since made his mark, the latter two having " passed brilliantly into the scientific branch of the British military service." Kipling's nickname was " Gigs " or " Giggsy," given him because of the huge glasses his near-sightedness forced him to wear. This affliction prevented his engaging actively in most athletic sports, though, in common with all his schoolmates, he was a good swimmer. He rambled much about the seashore, also, and was an adept in catching and training the young jackdaws which nested in the neighboring cliffs. The life at the college was of the most rough-and-tumble kind, floggings with cane and birch alternating with the laxest sort of discipline or absence of it, which resulted in the boys roaming over the country in predatory bands, poaching, fighting, and playing tricks on the farmers. While roguish rather than malicious, Rudyard seems to have been one of the most irrepressible of the lot, "always," as an old schoolmate tells us, "in some harmless mischief, always playing off some joke upon either one of his masters or his schoolfellows, no respecter of persons, and not caring one jot what good or evil opinion those held of him with whom he came in daily contact."

Young Kipling passed his holidays at South Kensington, in the home of his aunt, Mrs. Burne-Jones, where he became associated with men of the highest intellectual attainments, notably with William Morris, a close intimate of the family. The influence of such associations on the impressionable boy cannot easily be estimated.

4. JOURNALISM IN INDIA. — At the age of seventeen Kipling joined his parents in India, and through his father's influence obtained a position on the editorial staff of the Lahore *Civil and Military Gazette*. Here he served an apprenticeship of five years, leaving in 1887 to become assistant editor of the *Pioneer* at Allahabad. The latter position he held till 1889.

Perhaps the drudgery of a newspaper office, varied by missions to the frontier and to different parts of India, was the best possible preparation for his afterwork. Mr. Robinson, who has been previously quoted, was at this time the editor of the *Gazette*.

Of his young assistant he says: " My experience
of him as a newspaper hack suggests that if you want
to find a man who will cheerfully do the office work
of three men you should catch a young genius.
Like a blood horse between the shafts of a coal-
wagon, he may go near to bursting his heart in the
effort, but he'll drag that wagon along as it ought
to go.   The amount of 'stuff' that Kipling got
through in the day was indeed wonderful; and
though I had more or less satisfactory assistants after
he left, and the staff grew with the paper's prosperity, I am sure that more solid work was done in
that office when Kipling and I worked together than
ever before or after." [1]

But Kipling was far more than a drudge. Mr.
Robinson says further: " He was always the best of
good company, bubbling over with delightful humor,
which found vent in every detail of our day's work
together; and the chance visitor to the editor's office
must often have carried away very erroneous notions
of the amount of work which was being done when
he found us in the fits of laughter that usually accompanied our consultations about the make-up of
the paper." [2]

The astonishing local color in Kipling's tales is
the product of first-hand observation.   He neglected
no opportunity for gaining experience.   Natives of

---

[1] *McClure's*, July, 1896.
[2] *Ibid.*

all races and castes were known to him familiarly ; he
interviewed priests and fakirs ; he was a boon companion of Tommy Atkins ; he explored Chinese
opium-dens ; he absorbed the technical jargon of
popular sports; he mastered the details of the English administration ; he haunted the society of Mrs.
Hauksbee and her set in order to photograph on his
memory every gesture and every word.   At no time
in his life more than when in India did he justify Mr.
James Whitcomb Riley's apt characterization : " He
is a regular literary blotting-pad, soaking up everything on the face of the earth."

5. EARLY WRITINGS. — Young Kipling found
leisure outside of office hours to dash off short
stories and satirical ballads which appeared from
time to time in Indian newspapers and won immediate popularity.   As early as 1886 his name was
well known throughout India.   In this year the best
of the satirical verses were put together at Lahore in
" a sort of a book, a lean, oblong docket, to imitate a
Government envelope, bound in brown paper, and
tied with red tape."   It was not long before it
became a cloth-bound volume with gilt top, for several editions followed, but the author confesses to
have " loved it best when it was a little brown
baby with a pink string around his stomach."   So
rare is the first edition now that a copy in good
condition will fetch nearly or quite one hundred and
fifty dollars.

The year 1888 was one of extraordinary productiveness. Not fewer than seven books of prose fiction were published by Mr. Kipling. Of these the most noted if not the most notable is *Plain Tales from the Hills*. Before its publication the author had been popular and widely known; with its publication came fame.

6. AMERICAN TRIP. — But Mr. Kipling's fame was still confined almost wholly to Anglo-India. In 1889, sent by the *Pioneer*, to which he contributed entertaining letters of travel, he left India for England, armed with the slender volumes which had been printed in Lahore and Allahabad, and with manuscripts in which he had unbounded faith. He returned by way of Japan, San Francisco, and New York, thinking first to launch his literary ventures in the United States. In this he was disappointed. But if American publishers looked askance, his trip furnished pleasurable experiences and a liberal supply of "copy." Note-book in hand, he visited the Golden Gate and the Yellowstone; he explored Chicago, Salt Lake City, Buffalo, and New York. He fished for salmon in the Clackamas; he watched the evolutions of the United States army, and studied rural America at Musquash on the Monongahela. The *Pioneer* gives us the results of his impressions: the most bitterly satiric picture of American society which the world had seen since the publication of Dickens' *American Notes* in 1842.

7. LIFE IN LONDON. — The autumn of 1889 saw Mr. Kipling established in London fighting for recognition from the public. Although his stories found a publisher, they obtained almost no popular sale, until a favorable review in the *Times* (1890) brought him suddenly into notice. The most obscure author in London awoke to find himself the most talked of. The *World* pronounced him " the literary hero of the present hour." A friend who visited him at his chambers in the Strand discovered " a vast number of invitations from the best representative people of England lying on the table unanswered." It was literary not social success which he coveted. "I want to give good work," he said to a reporter of the *World*, " that is my only concern in life."

8. MARRIAGE. — In 1891 Mr. Kipling made a long voyage to South Africa, Australia, Ceylon, and New Zealand. In the same year he met in London Mr. Wolcott Balestier, the brilliant young American author with whom he afterward collaborated *The Naulahka*. He became acquainted also with Balestier's sister Caroline, between whom and himself there sprang up a strong friendship that ripened into love. They were married in London, Jan. 18, 1892.

Caroline Starr Balestier is the eldest daughter of the late H. Wolcott Balestier, of New York City, and comes of distinguished ancestry on both sides. Her maternal grandfather, the late Judge Peshine Smith, was said by William H. Seward to have a profounder knowledge of international law than any other living man.   It was Judge Smith who, on the recommendation of Seward, drafted for the Mikado of Japan commercial treaties between that nation and the great powers of the world.   His large fortune was left to his daughter, Mrs. Balestier, who holds it in trust for her six children.

The old family estate of the Balestiers (Beechwood) was in Brattleboro, Vt., and here, in the home of her grandparents, much of Mrs. Rudyard Kipling's girlhood was passed.   "A visit with her husband to these scenes of her childhood resulted in the selection of the site for their home among·the broad Balestier acres."

9. RESIDENCE IN THE UNITED STATES. — From August, 1892,to September, 1896, Mr. Kipling made his home in Brattleboro.   The young couple's first attempt at housekeeping was in the Bliss cottage, near the mansion of the Balestiers.   Here they lived while their new house was building.   The cottage is "a neat little white-clapboard, story-and-a-half fabric, which the novelist at first thought ' just large enough for two,' but which soon had a third occupant in the person of an infant daughter."   It was in this hillside cottage that some of the poems of the *Seven Seas* were written, that *Many Inventions* was completed, and the *Jungle Book* stories were begun.

But popular interest centres chiefly about the
Naulahka, Mr. Kipling's later house, and the only
one he ever built for himself. It is "a long, low,
two-storied frame bungalow of but a single room in
depth, whose dun hues blend and harmonize with
those of the hillside." [1]   A Brattleboro visitor writes,
" I went through the partly constructed Naulahka
and heard the owner describe its theory.   He called
it a ship, with the propeller, that is, the material
provision of the furnace and kitchen, at the stern,
and his own study, opening upon the roomy piazza
looking to the south and east, at the bow." [2]

It was in his capacious study at the Naulahka
that many of Mr. Kipling's finest poems and short
stories were written, as well as the whole of the
Gloucester fishing-tale — " Captains Courageous."

10. ENGLAND AND SOUTH AFRICA. —On leaving Vermont, Mr. Kipling returned to England and
took a house for a short time at Torquay.   Early in
1898 the poet with his family made a tour to Cape
Town, South Africa, where his greeting from the
English population was exceedingly warm.   He removed in the spring of this year to his present home,
Rottingdean, Sussex, a village near Brighton.   His
place is called " The Elms," from the superb trees
surrounding it.   Here Mr. Kipling has led a quiet,
retired life, keeping in good form for his literary

---

[1] Wolfe's *Literary Haunts and Homes.*
[2] The Rev. C. O. Day, in *Congregationalist.*

labor by a three-hours' morning ride and a walk of five or six miles later in the day. His evenings are frequently passed at the village inn, where he smokes with the landlord and discusses politics.

The autumn of 1898 brought Mr. Kipling an opportunity for observing the Royal Navy at close range. On the invitation of one of the commanding officers he enjoyed a cruise with the Channel Squadron around the coast of Ireland ; this resulted in the series of brilliant descriptive letters contributed to the London *Morning Post* under the title " A Fleet in Being."

11. VISIT TO AMERICA AND ILLNESS. — In the latter part of January, 1899, Mr. Kipling sailed for America with his family, intending to make a short stay in New York and Washington, after which he purposed to visit Mexico. He arrived February 2, and had hardly become settled in New York before he began to suffer from a serious cold which refused to be shaken off. On the 20th he was taken suddenly ill with an inflammation of the lungs that developed rapidly into " double " pneumonia. Everything was done for the poet which medical science and the loving care of his wife could devise, but he grew worse, and for a number of days was kept alive only by the administration of oxygen. He was, most of the time, unconscious. Dr. Janeway, the well-known New York specialist, and Dr. Dunham who married Miss Josephine Balestier,

Mrs. Kipling's younger sister, had charge of the
case, and were unwearying in their attentions.   The
sick man's apartments were at the Grenoble, and
the hotel corridors were crowded with anxious
friends, while a stream of telegrams and cable-dis-
patches poured in upon Mrs. Kipling.   New York
and Boston dailies devoted their leading columns to
discussing the case, and the London papers issued
extras for every bulletin.   Max Eliot, the London
correspondent, wrote: " In the streets the only cry
of the newsboys is, ' Latest reports of Rudyard Kipling.' " The German Kaiser sent the following dis-
patch to the author's wife :

BERLIN, March 5.

MRS. RUDYARD KIPLING, *Hotel Grenoble :*

As an enthusiastic admirer of the unrivalled books of your
husband, I am most anxious for news about his health.   God
grant that he may be spared to you and to all who are thankful
to him for the soul-stirring way in which he has sung about the
deeds of our great common race.

WILLIAM, I. R.

The crisis in the disease was passed in the morning of March first ; a slight gain in a resolution of
the lower lobes could be reported, and the patient
dropped into his first refreshing sleep for days.

12. DEATH OF MR. KIPLING'S DAUGHTER. —
Meantime Elsie and Josephine, Mr. Kipling's little
daughters, had fallen ill with pneumonia.   Elsie,
the younger, had recovered, but on March 6
Josephine, a six-year-old, and the eldest of Mr.

Kipling's three children, died at the home of a family friend whither she had been removed early in her illness. The child's death was carefully concealed from her father for several days, and all matters connected with the funeral were, in accordance with Mrs. Kipling's earnest wish, kept entirely private. The doctors finally decided to break the news, since the worry which the patient exhibited about the little one's whereabouts and welfare was deemed to be more dangerous than the truth. " Tears stood in the poet's eyes," says a contemporary account, " and he murmured, half to himself, half aloud: ' Poor little Joe.' "

13. RESTORATION TO HEALTH. — Despite the sorrow of this great bereavement, Mr. Kipling suffered no relapse, though his improvement was very slow. By the second of April he was out of bed and well on the road to recovery. It was on that day that he gave to the press the following letter of thanks:

HOTEL GRENOBLE, EASTER DAY, 1899.

DEAR SIR: Will you allow me through your columns to attempt some acknowledgment of the wonderful sympathy, affection, and kindness shown towards me during my recent illness, as well as the unfailing courtesy that controlled its expression ? I am not strong enough to answer letters in detail, so I must take this means of thanking, as humbly as sincerely, the countless people of good will throughout the world who have put me under a debt I can never hope to repay.

Faithfully yours,
RUDYARD KIPLING.

In the latter part of June Mr. Kipling and his family returned to their English home.

14. PERSONALITY. — In appearance Mr. Kipling is a little under average stature, with a compact figure and a slight stoop. Behind the spectacles, worn to correct astigmatism, gleam a pair of kind and alert eyes. In more than one respect Rudyard Kipling the child was the father of Rudyard Kipling the man. The following description of the poet as he looked in the early summer of 1879 was contributed to the San Francisco *Examiner* by Mr. George Arnold Wilkie, an old classmate:

" Picture to yourself a chunky, open-faced boy of about fourteen years. He was very brown from his residence in India, and he had thick black hair, rather inclined to be curly. His jaw was strong, his teeth large and very white. He had a rolling gait, and walked with his fists crammed in the pockets of his coat. He was a fairly good tennis player, and I know he used to grieve at his near-sightedness, which prevented him from excelling in the sport. As a boy Kipling was notably careless in dress. He would not comb and brush his thick hair carefully, and he had a habit of going with his shoe laces untied. He loved to fish all by himself, or, at any rate, with only one companion, and he would come home to his immaculate mother and sister with a mass of dock burrs or several varieties of nettles clinging to his clothes in a dozen places, while fish scales stuck to his coat and trousers like postage stamps." [1]

Mr. Robinson's first impression of the poet is worth reprinting. "With Kipling himself I was disappointed at first. At the time of which I am writing, early in 1886, his face had not acquired the character of manhood, and contrasted somewhat unpleasantly with his stoop (acquired through much bending over an office table), his heavy eyebrows, his spectacles, and his sallow Anglo-Indian complexion, while his jerky speech and abrupt movements added to the unfavorable impression. But his conversation was brilliant, and his sterling character gleamed through the humorous light which shone behind his spectacles, and in ten minutes he fell into his natural place as the most striking member of a remarkably clever and charming family." A reporter for the London *World* described Mr. Kipling in 1890 as "a short, but broadly-figured man, dark, with blue eyes and a resolute jaw, still quite young, — he is not yet twenty-five, — but with a face on which time and incident have prematurely traced many tell-tale marks." A more recent scribe has this: "I happened to dine at the same table with him at the hotel, and though I recognized him from portraits which I had seen, I might have done so from the

[1] Condensed from an abstract of the article in *Current Literature* for April, 1899.

constant play of comment from him as his eye fell
on every little object in the room with the liveliest
curiosity."

Mr. Kipling is a fair draughtsman, a clever amateur actor, a remarkable conversationist, a gracious
host, — though of freezing manners toward the im-
pertinent and curious, — and a royal entertainer of
children. Of children he has said that he who can
reach the child's heart can reach the world's heart.
In athletics and out-of-door games he has the keen-
est interest, though he plays more like an enthusiastic amateur than a professional sportsman. During
the winter — at any rate when in Vermont — he
coasts, snow-shoes, " skis," plays golf upon the
crust, and shovels out the paths and walks ; in summer he wheels, tramps, cultivates a garden, or
fishes. More deservedly than to almost any living
author does the hackneyed phrase " an all-round
man " apply to Mr. Rudyard Kipling.

15. PORTRAITS. — Among the familiar portraits
of Mr. Kipling may be named (1) The Bourne
and Shepherd (Simla) photograph, taken when the
author was about twenty years of age ; (2) the El-
liott and Fry (London) photograph, perhaps the
most widely known ; (3) the painting by the Hon.
John Collier, exhibited in the Royal Academy,
1891 ; (4) the celebrated colored woodcut litho-
graph made by Mr. William Nicholson for the *New
Review*, and published by Heinemann in England,

and R. H. Russell in New York (standing posture); (5) the drawing by the Marchioness of Granby (profile, without glasses); (6) the etching by William Strang from life (profile, arms folded); (7 and 8) the portrait frontispieces to *The Courting of Dinah Shadd*, *Harper's*, and to the *Outward Bound* edition of works, *Scribner's*.

CHAPTER TWO

I

1. THE STAR IN THE EAST.— Mr. Kipling's advent into the world of letters occurred at a very fortunate moment. Both critics and public were weary of the burrowing analysis which had come to supplant a healthy love of incident and a regard for plot. Microscopic dissection of motives and the photography of hard-featured men and women formed the staple of contemporary fiction. Combined with this uncompromising realism was an excessive refinement of language, evasive and self-conscious. It was at this juncture that Mr. Kipling presented the English people with his brusque, unhackneyed stories of " a cleaner, greener land," and found an audience eager to welcome him.

2. THE ZENITH OF FAME. — Fifteen years ago Rudyard Kipling's name was unknown in India; ten years ago it was unknown in England. To-day Mr. Kipling's fame is international. William Dean Howells has said in a recent interview : " I am honestly of the opinion that Kipling is the most famous man in the world to-day. . . . In fact I think it

(32)

fair to say that Kipling's reputation is greater than that of any English-speaking poet who ever lived." How can this most meteor-like of literary reputations be accounted for?

3. Can We Account for Kipling's Vogue? — Mr. Kipling's popularity may be attributed to the romantic conception of a "young Lochinvar of fiction, who came out of the East, came unannounced, and came all alone." It may be attributed to his contemporaneousness — his vital interest in what the world is talking about, whether it be the Queen's Jubilee, America's policy in the Philippines, or the Czar's Proclamation. We may say it is due to his celebration of machinery, and of nineteenth century exploration and enterprise, or to his flattery of British national pride. But such answers are superficial. Other versifiers and tale-writers have struck the same notes; our newspapers are full of timely poems which are either left unread, or read once and forgotten. Other writers, too, have made entrances on the literary stage which have been almost as dramatic. Wide-spread popularity may be won by many qualities: world-wide fame has never yet been, and never will be, won except by a union of qualities deserving to be called great. What gives Mr. Kipling's work the character of greatness?

4. Why Kipling may be Called Great. — Mr. Kipling's work may properly be called great because he has so much to say, and knows so well

how to say it. He combines and coördinates message and style.

This combination may at first thought seem common enough. A second thought convinces one of the contrary. Who remembers nine-tenths of current magazine verse? With all their gift for saying things, most magazine poets have nothing to say. At any event, they have nothing new to say. They give us graceful prettiness and millinery, but offer little to our intellects, and nothing to our immortal souls. On the other hand, many earnest men have something to tell us, but are inarticulate from lack of training, or at best are stammering, hoarse-voiced, and full of awkward gestures. Here at last comes a man who, it would seem, has been everywhere, observed everything, arrived at the meaning of his discoveries, and knows also how to make us perceive with our own eyes what he has viewed with his — a man, in a word, who has both matter and manner.

5. MESSAGE AND STYLE ANALYZED. — Mr. Kipling's body of thought is of the highest importance, because it combines truth, human interest, and variety; his style is of the highest value, because it combines force with precision.

6. MESSAGE: *Truth.* — No work of literature can be of lasting importance if its fundamental conception is based upon an untruth. Many of Mr. Ruskin's charmingly written papers fall short of the

highest importance because based on false proposi-
tions. This may be said also of some of Carlyle's
later pamphlets, of certain of Mr. Arnold's theolog-
ical essays, of not a few of Mr. Swinburne's poems,
and of such books as *Queen Mab*, and James
Thomson's *City of Dreadful Night*. No amount of
brilliant expression can compensate for radically
false views of human nature and of society. Now
it may be said of Mr. Kipling's work as a whole
that while the facts he selects are often novel or
exceptional, they are based on truths of human
nature as old as Job or Homer. Vice never triumphs permanently over virtue, and it bears its
proper punishment. True, Mr. Kipling loves to
show us that the sinner has something of the saint
about him, and the saint is not all saint; but he
never confuses moral values. In politics he guards
against *laisser-faire* on the one hand, tyranny and
toryism on the other. Mr. Kipling has that sober
accuracy of vision that apprehends things in their
relations.

7. MESSAGE : *Human Interest*. — The value
of a story-teller's work depends largely on the
amount and quality of the human life he can depict. Mr. Kipling's work deserves to be taken
seriously, because, in the first place, it gives us so
much of life; because, in the second place, it gives
us so much of the noble, invigorating side of life.
While realistic in method, it is ideal in aim.

Our author's heroes

" Are neither children nor gods, but men in a world of men."[1]

The delight in mere physical struggle, the love of
home and equal love of roving adventure, the friendship of man for man, the remorse which follows
wasted opportunities, jealousy, hatred, and revenge
— where are these primary qualities of our nature
given more powerful expression ?   The words Mr.
Kipling once applied to Wressley apply quite as
truly to himself: " His heart and soul were at the
end of his pen, and they got into the ink.   He was
dowered with sympathy, insight, humor, and style
for two hundred and thirty days and nights; and his
book was a Book.   He had his vast special knowledge with him, so to speak ; but the spirit, the woven-
in human touch, the poetry and the power of the
output, were beyond all special knowledge."[2]   Mr.
Kipling's work is a cross-section through nineteenth-
century society from Supi-yaw-lat to the Widow of
Windsor, from Gunga Din to the Viceroy.   He is
interested in one thing and one alone.   It is not
nature, theology, life even — but lives.   Not humanity, but Dick, Tom, and Harry; not human
nature, but your nature; not the brotherhood of
man, but Gunga Din, Disco Troop, McAndrew,
his brothers.   The subject that cannot be related

---

[1] "A Song of the English."
[2] Wressley of the Foreign Office.

to the real experience of a real man has no charm for him.

But the human nature to which Mr. Kipling introduces us is not only vigorous and varied: it is wholesome.[1] No side of human nature is without interest for him ; but the most fascinating side is that which struggles for the attainment of ideal ends. We drop his books with more faith rather than less in men and women. Bobby Wicks is far removed from the saint, but he dies for a comrade and makes no fuss about it. Hummil, too, has the minor vices of his class, but he sacrifices his life for another. Jakin and Lew are children of the gutter, but they die drumming and fifing defiantly far in advance of the cowardly regiment. To say that the author's sympathies are not universal is only to say that they are healthy. He detests the prig, and hates above all the religious prig. The Pharisee, whether called by the name of Mrs. Jennett, or Antirosa, or Riley the bank accountant, or Mrs. Scriffshaw, he has no good word for. But towards the imperfect men and women who do the

---

[1] A few of the early stories and ballads hardly deserve this praise. Yet the savagery of Kipling's satiric mood was wakened only by what he felt to be cant, hypocrisy, or cowardice. If he saw cant, hypocrisy, and cowardice where they do not exist, the error lay in his defective judgment and undeveloped faculty of sympathy, not in heart and will. Mr. Kipling's pessimism, moreover, was far from indicating moral apathy. Had he cared nothing for ethics, had he possessed no private standard of conduct, he would have been either indifferent to wrong or oblivious to it.

day's work with brave patience and a bold heart —
toward

"Such as praise our God for that they served His world,"

Mr. Kipling's interest and sympathy are undevi-
ating.

8. MESSAGE : *Variety.* — The value of literature depends in part on its range. A man who sees
a few things or knows a single place is obviously
less well-equipped for story-writing than a man who
has observed very widely. This is not because one
place offers less valuable material than another. It
is partly because any theme, however interesting,
becomes wearisome if harped on ; it is also because
a man needs to see a good many things before he
can gauge the proper proportions of any one thing.

One of the most astonishing merits of Mr. Kipling is his range. He has laid the scenes of his
tales in India, South Africa, the United States, the
Newfoundland Banks, the East End of London,
English country villages, mid-ocean, and the islands
of the sea. He has written children's tales, mystery
tales, soldier stories, beast fables, humorous and
sailor yarns, studies in native Indian life, sporting
tales, and society dialogues. He writes fluently in
every dialect under heaven. While his stories of
India are mainly concerned with four classes, —
British soldiers, fashionable Anglo-Indian society,
children of British officials, and natives, — his later

tales include London bank-clerks, Gloucester fishermen, California millionaires, New York journalists, and Devonshire schoolboys. When he essays verse he is equally resourceful. Most poets can be classed by their little fields, as poets of heroism, of adventure, of the sea, of the army, of politics. Mr. Kipling is the poet of all this and of how much beside! In *The Seven Seas* he writes of the British empire, of the English soldier, of the American spirit, of the three-volume novel, of the sea fight between the sealing boats, of the cave-dwellers, of the true romance. Mr. James Whitcomb Riley writes of Kipling : " He has the greatest curiosity of any man I ever knew ; everything interests him." He knows the name of every rope on the Newfoundland fishing schooner, and writes with equal mastery of a Greek galley, Chinese pig-boat, Bilbao tramp, British man-of-war, and Atlantic liner. " Mr. Kipling's accuracy is phenomenal," says a *Popular Science Monthly* writer in discussing *The Scientific Spirit in Kipling's Work*. Read the *Jungle Books*, and see how intimate is his knowledge of zoölogy, the *Story of Ung* and *In the Neolithic Age*, and observe his familiar acquaintance with archeology. In *Quiquern* and *The White Seal* he shows the same easy mastery of Arctic exploration, in *The Flowers* of botany, in *The English Flag* of geography, in *The Children of the Zodiac* of the constellations.

9. STYLE : *Force.* — The word *beautiful* would never come to mind if one were asked to characterize the work of Mr. Kipling in a single epithet. What we first notice about him is his power. He means something and means it hard. It is impossible to ignore him; his demand is too immediate and persistent. Read where you will, his writings strike you "with the weight of a six-fold blow." "His vitality and force are so extraordinary that they sweep the goddess of Criticism off her legs," said a eulogist in the *Saturday Review.* Let the reader once get caught in the dash and swing of *The Seven Seas* and he is swept along irresistibly until *finis* at the book's end casts him ashore again half-drowned but happy. When a man can bring this about, only the purist, the grammarian, or the prig will question whether he is a poet. We recommend to all such Mr. Kipling's "Conundrum of the Workshops":

"They builded a tower to shiver the sky and wrench the stars apart,
   Till the devil grunted behind the bricks : 'It's striking, but is it art ?' "

Art may be crude or coarse, but it is successful if it achieve its purpose. If the artist's product "strikes" you, art of some sort it certainly is. The distinguishing characteristic of wholly inartistic things is this: They do not strike one at all.

10. STYLE : *Precision.* — In addition to force

style should have precision. Macaulay possesses force, but so little delicacy that he constantly understates or overstates his meaning. He chooses primary colors and has no subtlety of shading. On the other hand, Mr. Pater and Mr. James cultivate precision of phrase, one thinks, at the expense of energy. What makes Mr. Kipling's use of language so triumphantly successful is the fact that he combines strength and exactness, almost never sacrificing one to the other. The *Spectator* has said of him that he " is of all living writers the most careful and conscientious in the matter of form." He knows the value of individual words as a mechanic knows the use and importance of different tools, and can turn with perfect ease from the sledge-hammer to the awl or file. In his powerful and odd, though wholly serious, conception of the Hereafter, the happy artist " shall splash at a ten-league canvas with brushes of comet's hair." But the splashes are not daubs. Kipling hastens to add that the painter " shall draw the thing as he sees it, for the God of Things as They Are." [1]

Such a coördination of vigor and nicety is very remarkable. It is Byron and Mr. Aldrich in partnership.

---

[1] L'envoi to *The Seven Seas.*

II

11. MR. KIPLING'S THREE PERIODS. — Mr. Kipling's work may be divided for convenience into three periods : Satirical Treatment of Character; Sympathetic Treatment of Character; Spiritual Treatment of Character.

12. SATIRICAL TREATMENT OF CHARACTER.— In Mr. Kipling's early writings one hears the sound of scornful laughter. There is irony, wit, cleverness in plenty, but a lack of the charity which " suffereth long and is kind."

The first book which deserves consideration is *Departmental Ditties*, a collection of verses mainly satirical and almost wholly concerned with Indian official life. It is impossible for outside readers to appreciate, as the little Anglo-Indian world of the eighties could, all the allusions to Delilah, Boanerges Blitzen, Pagett, M.P., and Potiphar Gubbins. Yet these queer appellations stood for the names of men and women widely known in the circles the poet frequented, and the sharp personalities struck home. The book enjoyed the same sort of success that topical songs filled with local " gags " always win at vaudeville theatres. It was in some sense a survival of the mood which led the schoolboy Kipling to lampoon his masters, but it had perhaps a more serious intent. The occasional pieces are certain to be forgotten, since their appeal is to passing, not permanent, sources of interest. The society verse is already forgotten, since this above all kinds of poetry demands perfectly polished form — precisely the point where the youthful Kipling was deficient. A few of the *Ditties*, however, deserve to survive.

One of them is " The Story of Uriah," an Anglo-Indian version of the David and Bathsheba narrative. It is unpleasant, it has no smoothness or charm, but every word is like a blow of the fist.

Another poem which gives earnest of Mr. Kipling's maturer style is " The Galley Slave," an allegorical description of the Indian Civil Service. It preaches a robust gospel from first line to last :

> " Was it storm ? Our fathers faced it, and a wilder never
> blew ;
> Earth that waited for the wreckage watched the galley struggle through."

Perhaps still finer is the jubilee poem, " What the People Said " :

> " By the well, where the bullocks go
> Silent and blind and slow."

It has just that added note of spirituality which is wanting in the rest of the book, and points prophetically to the " Recessional " of a decade later.

As a whole, the tone of these *Ditties* is disagreeable. Their attitude toward life is very juvenile. Here is a sample :

"Open the old cigar-box — let me consider anew —
Old friends, and who is Maggie that I should abandon
you ?"

"A million surplus Maggies are willing to bear the yoke :
And a woman is only a woman, but a good cigar is a
smoke."

No plea of deliberate humor excuses such brutal
cynicism.

Another representative work of this early period
is *Plain Tales from the Hills.* Here we find much
the same merits and faults as in *Departmental Ditties.*
The tales are notable for force, conciseness, unity,
and wit. They have a spontaneousness about them
which some of Mr. Kipling's very recent stories
lack. They were not written to propitiate the critics, nor to win money, nor to satisfy his own mature
and exacting canons of taste. They were dashed
off to please himself. They are consequently
marked by an astounding freshness and charm,
and even the poorest of them has the quality of
being readable. What they lack is that sympathetic insight which delves beneath surface faults of
character and discovers the fountains of human suf-
fering. Many of them are marred by cynicism,
nearly all of them by cocksureness — the jaunty hat-
on-one-side, chip-on-shoulder air of precocious
youth. The best of the stories are those in which Mr.
Kipling drops his air of knowingness, and is content
to stand aside and let his story tell itself, as he does

in that masterpiece of humor " The Taking of
Lungtungpen," and that masterpiece of pathos —
probably the finest thing in the book — " The
Story of Muhammad Din."

In *Under the Deodars* Kipling's effort is to depict
the shallow fashionable society of Simla.   Here his
cynical temper finds chance for complete expression.
It is not the fact that so many of these stories turn
on the motive of adultery to which one objects.   It
is the fact that we are not given a clear perspective.
Mr. Barrie defends Kipling for " choosing the dirty
corner."   He finds fault, however, with good
reason, because " the blaze of light is always on the
one spot : we never see the rest of the room."[1]

By what right does the author direct the rays of
his lantern on unfaithful husbands and intriguing
wives without allowing us to observe the thousands
of excellent British subjects in India who cultivate
the old-fashioned virtues ?   It is true that Mr. Kipling writes of immorality in a moral way; he never
makes it seductive, nor fails to show that it bears its
penalty.   He misplaces his accent, that is all.   Con-
ceding him a perfect right to " draw the Thing as he
sees it," we still regret that " whatsoever things are
pure, whatsoever things are lovely, whatsoever
things are of good report " are not, in these early
stories, given quite a fair chance.

The satiric spirit is hardly less prominent in the

[1] *Contemporary Review.*

Story of the Gadsbys, a series of social studies with
the cynical moral that a soldier married is a soldier
marred:

"Down to Gehenna or up to the Throne
He travels the fastest who travels alone." [1]

Gadsby himself has this to say to Captain Mafflim:
"Jack, be very sure of yourself before you marry.
I'm an ungrateful ruffian to say this, but marriage
— even as good a marriage as mine has been —
hampers a man's work, it cripples his sword-arm,
and oh, it plays Hell with his notions of duty!"
The lack of genuine chivalry toward women has
always been one of Mr. Kipling's faults, but it has
never elsewhere touched the depths it reaches in
these Gadsby dialogues. Much can be forgiven
the author on the score of his extreme youth. But
can that excuse be stretched to cover the retention
of this book in the *Outward Bound* edition, recently
revised by the author? The *Story of the Gadsbys* is
as superficial and vulgar in tone as it is brilliant in
composition, and can add nothing to the author's
fame.

Another representative work of this early period
is *The Light that Failed*, Mr. Kipling's first novel.
It has powerful passages, but lacks tolerance and
sanity. It is a very young book. Its air of om-
niscience becomes tiresome; its violence is never
felt, except in the superb battle passages, to be

[1] L'envoi to *Story of the Gadsbys*.

exactly vigor. As a story it is disheartening. In reviewing it the *Quarterly* reminded Mr. Kipling of a forgotten truth: "The finest art is full of light and hope." It subordinates "other qualities, however brilliant, to a belief in the best things about God and man." Dick Heldar's blindness seems, in view of his character, "more like retribution than like Nemesis." Pity him as much as we may, we would have pitied him more if his spirit from the first had been less magisterial and selfish, if he had not been so resentful of an affront to his pride and so contemptuous of the common herd who would have none of art. Dick had yet to learn, like Mr. Kipling himself, that even shop-keepers and Sunday-school superintendents should possess an interest for a broadly receptive mind; that very lovable people have been known to attend dissenting chapels and to prefer religious tracts to Shakespeare's plays. When Dick Heldar gains his first sight of London after returning from the Soudan he addresses the following speech to a row of highly respectable houses: "'Oh, you rabbit-hutches! Do you know what you've got to do later on? You have to supply me with men-servants and maid-servants,' — here he smacked his lips, — 'and the peculiar treasure of kings. Meantime I'll get clothes and boots, and presently I will return and trample on you.'" Surely that is not the mental temper which makes either for Christianity or for good art.

The work of Mr. Kipling's first period, then, is
marked by dash, wit, and inexhaustible cleverness,
but is marred by the characteristic faults of youth :
lack of sympathy and undeveloped sense of propor-
tion.

13. SYMPATHETIC TREATMENT OF CHARACTER.
— But the author had already begun to promise
better things.   As interpretations of the queer
workings of the Oriental mind and still queerer
workings of the all but impenetrable native conscience, some of the stories in *In Black and White*
are unparalleled.   In certain tales of *Soldiers Three*,
and in at least one of the child stories, he touched
almost the highest level he has reached.   The reason
is obvious.   He was writing of the classes of people
with whom he was in complete *rapport*, and he was
attempting to vindicate no favorite theory of art or
society.   Human nature was treated in a broader
spirit which made its appeal less and less to the
passing interest evoked by clever description of class
manners and social fashions and more to the permanent interest awakened by portrayal of primitive
and lasting emotions.

A very fortunate field for the exercise of his
talents was offered by the ballads of 1892.   Mr.
Kipling no longer gave us society as he had found
it, or sin as he had unearthed it, or art as he chose
to preach it ;   he set Tommy Atkins to singing and
let him relate his own story to music.   The result

is perhaps the faithfullest picture of the common soldier we have in modern literature. Of the gallant officer-on-leave, of the picturesque veteran, or of a sort of sentimentalized man-in-the-ranks, conceived either as lover or as simon-pure hero, fiction gives us many examples. But the " snoring Barrack-room," cholera scourge, canteen, commissariat " camuels," battery mules, sweating carriers, " 'arf-made recruities " — these seem to have been reserved for Rudyard Kipling. The poet never ventriloquizes. We are not asked to believe that a young journalist masquerading in a red coat is Mr. Atkins. Never once does the singer of the Barrack-room stand off and view his soldier-man with cynical or even with merely curious while friendly interest ; he sleeps under the same blanket, he smokes the same tobacco, he shares the same rations, he gets near enough to his comrade's heart to discover the rude chivalry which redeems his undisguised animalism. The common man of the British army is at last completely realized.

In the prose tales of Mr. Kipling's second period one sees not only surer mastery of form and the sloughing off of mannerisms ; even more apparent is the growth in sympathy. There is not a page in the *Plain Tales*, unless we except " The Story of Muhammad Din," that reveals anything approaching the tenderness of the tale entitled " Without Benefit of Clergy." " Beyond the Pale " has, to be sure, a plot

which presents similarities, yet that pitiful little narrative is, after all, a study from the outside ; it fails to
seize the heartstrings like Ameera's story.   It is plain
enough that the situation could never have been
entered into with the same absorption by the
author. " Love-o'-Women," too, in *Many Inventions*,
grips the sympathies as none of the early tales do.
The same may be said of several stories of this
middle period.   They are not the notes of a jour-
nalist-observer ; they are a serious man's record of
the points of view and mental sufferings of other
minds.   The composition of " The Destroyer of
Traffic," for example, is possible only to a writer of
no little dramatic sympathy and capacity for self-
detachment.   All the jauntiness of the early writings has now vanished.   The tone is manly,
wholesome, optimistic.   The humor is kinder, the
pathos less strained ; the wise humility of maturity
has succeeded the flippancy of youth.

    14. SPIRITUAL TREATMENT OF CHARACTER.—
If the temper of Mr. Kipling's first period was
satiric and that of his second period dramatic, that
of his third may be called philosophic.   It is a
remarkable evolution.   While Mr. Kipling is a
charming story-teller still (he is nothing if not artist),
the reader is impressed by a growing undercurrent
of allegory and symbolism.   In the *Jungle Tales*
the author sets man over against the background of
nature, shows us the inferiority of the overcivilized

and house-bred man to the natural man, and of
human society, in more than one particular, to
brute society. Is not the "Law of the Jungle"
"the reproof of human codes in its comprehensive
justice"? "*Captains Courageous*," too, is one long
parable on the relation of character to environment.
The Day's Work is an elaborate piece of symbolism,
standing for the tremendous conflict of man with
the forces of nature and of circumstance. The
struggle may be against the wrath of a flood, as in
"The Bridge-Builders," or against a relentless famine, as in "William the Conqueror." The struggle
may be that of the social unit to adjust itself to the
needs of the social organization, as in the allegory
called "The Ship that Found Herself," — everywhere, however, it is conflict of will with will or of
force with force. "I like men who do things," confesses William the Conqueror. All the men in *The
Day's Work* do things, all the horses and locomotives
and marine engines do things. Mr. Kipling's philosophy of life is summed up in this sentence from
"The Bridge-Builders" : "The order in all cases was
to stand by the day's work and wait instructions."
The duty of struggle, the duty of obedience —
these are the two articles in this strenuous creed.
"It's all in the day's work," says Scott in "William
the Conqueror." "It's all in the day's run," says
.007 in the locomotive story. "Play the game —
don't talk," whickers the "Maltese Cat." The *Jungle*

Books stand for the struggle for supremacy between natural and artificial forces. " *Captains Courageous* " teaches the necessity of learning to take orders. This, too, is the lesson McAndrew obtains from his engines —

" Law, Orrder, Duty an' Restraint, Obedience, Discipline." Discipline, however, is only to the end of more effective activity. We obey orders that we may catch more cod on the Banks or make a quicker run to port.

Most of the poetry is of the same timbre. If the prose taken together is an epic which sings the eternal struggle of man to survive against the powers which war against his body and soul, such poems as " The Song of the English " and most of the others in varying degree sing the struggle for race-survival between the conquering Saxons and their rivals. It may be said that one gets in certain recent writings the note of reverence and humility —

> " Still stands Thine ancient sacrifice,
> An humble and a contrite heart."

Such submission, however, is not opposed to the gospel of endeavor; it is a part of it. It is Cromwell's sort of submission — the stooping of the soldier to buckle on his armor. In the light of " The Truce of the Bear " and " The White Man's Burden," which followed the " Recessional " and to some degree interpreted it, we cannot doubt that while

> " The captains and the kings depart,"

they don't depart to their homes and become trades-people. Instead of laying down their weapons they sleep upon them. One of Mr. Kipling's sturdy heroes confesses, " The Lord abideth back of me to guide my fighting-arm." This is the sort of deity Mr. Kipling invokes. Indeed, his conception of God is more Hebraic than Christian. God is represented in his writings as either the " Lord God of Battles," or the " Master of all Good Workmen." The obedience to God which Kipling enjoins is the sort of obedience which he recommends for Harvey Cheyne in " *Captains Courageous* " — that obedience which enables the boy by submitting himself to the commands of the skipper to work to better result himself. It is significant that the term Mr. Kipling selects for the Deity in his remarkable invocation which concludes *Life's Handicap* is " Great Overseer." In his poem addressed to Wolcott Balestier he makes reference to " Our wise Lord God, master of every trade." Not only does Mr. Kipling transfer his conception of effort to the future life where we shall labor " each for the joy of the working," but he makes faithful work on earth the price of admission both to heaven and Hades. Gunga Din, cut off in mid-career, dies in the performance of duty. He will be permitted to finish his task in " the place where 'e is gone." It is not Gunga Din, but the milk and water Tomlinson who is refused admission in turn to heaven and hell because unable to answer the test, "What ha' ye done?"

But the poet has for his end neither the satisfaction of fighting — the glow of the muscles — nor the accomplishment of vulgar success. McAndrew, the Scotch engineer, who takes comfort in reflecting, "I *am* o' service to my kind. Ye wadna' blame the thought," echoes Mr. Kipling's own creed. Even in the earliest of his long stories he writes, "If we make light of our work, by using it for our own ends, our work will make light of us." And again, "You're on the wrong road to success. It isn't got at by sacrificing other people, — I've had that much knocked into me; you must sacrifice yourself, and live under orders." The closing lines of one of his most devout poems breathe the same spirit:

" One stone the more swings to her place
  In that dread Temple of Thy Worth;
It is enough that through Thy grace
  I saw naught common on Thy earth.

" Take not that vision from my ken;
  Oh, whatsoe'er may spoil or speed,
Help me to need no aid from men
  That I may help such men as need." [1]

To such a vision, what is commonly called failure seems unimportant. Is not Mr. Kipling him-

---

[1] L'envoi to *Life's Handicap*.

self speaking behind the mask of the talking banjo :

" I have known Defeat, and mocked it as we ran " ?

This is the sort of faith to which anything less than success appears inconceivable.

But valiant and uncompromising as it is, this creed lacks the one thing essential to completeness. In making duty, not love, the motive power to action, especially when that action is viewed in the light of service to others, Mr. Kipling ignores the highest sanction for the day's work. In this he is the antithesis of Robert Browning and of St. John, and the very brother-in-blood of Mr. Thomas Çarlyle. Like the sage of Chelsea, he has failed to say the last word on his theme.

For love — even the love that is mixed with earth — Mr. Kipling finds little place in his gospel. Thomas Atkins says of the London " 'ousemaids " that " they talks a lot o' lovin', but wot do they understand ? " Few of Kipling's characters understand much, though many lovers are included in his repertory. Love, in our author's thought, is a very delightful incident of the day's work, but the building of bridges and engines and empires ministers, after all, rather more to the growth of character and of civilization. Not many midday hours must be devoted to wooing, though it is an admirable amusement for evenings when one cannot

labor out o' doors. One of Kipling's characters
" held peculiar notions as to the wooing of girls.
He said that the best work of a man's career should
be laid reverently at their feet." Kipling adds,
" Ruskin writes something like this somewhere, I
think ; but in ordinary life a few kisses are better
and save time." Love, in Kipling's thought, is
not a passion to abandon one's self to. Only little
Hindu widows or very callow subalterns make
this blunder, and they always pay for it. I cannot
but feel that Kipling always has a slight tone of
patronage toward women. The women whom he
really likes are those who have most of the masculine grafted into their natures. They are either
clever in argument, like Mrs. Hauksbee, or able
to " rule eight servants and two horses," like
" William the Conqueror." Love, it is true,
forms the basis of very many of Kipling's stories.
But it will be noted that his interest is not in the
sentiment or the passion itself, but in the compli-
cations growing therefrom.

   If Mr. Kipling finds small place for passionate
love he finds almost none for spiritual love. I have
already intimated that the tenderness of the All
Father means less to him than the power of the All
Ruler. " The Lord is a just and terrible God,
Bess," Dick Heldar explains. That seems to be the
view of Mulholland, of McAndrew, of all the militant saints of these ballads and stories. Marked as

is the growth of religious insight in Mr. Kipling's recent writings, the years have still much to teach him. He has sung of obedience and work, none more nobly; may we not hope that he will yet rise to the Apostolic conception : "The greatest of these is Love" ?

III

GENERAL CHARACTERISTICS

15. ORIGINALITY. — Mr. Kipling seems never to have imitated anybody. He has been compared to Bret Harte, to Pierre Loti, to Dickens. But the truth is, he owes practically nothing to other writers. He formed himself on no classic models, but relied for inspiration solely upon " that Light which lighteth every man that cometh into the world." He is as truly a successful original as Carlyle or Browning or Walt Whitman.

His originality is shown first of all in his choice of theme. Politicians and compilers of statistics wrote about India for centuries, but the novelists passed it by. A young man, picking up the discarded material, taught the world more about the Orient than all histories and blue-books, and " brought India nearer to England than the Suez Canal has done." He has made us see India, and feel it, and smell it.

He has dared also to write of the common soldier,

who, for the most part, had been overlooked by the
novelists and poets, and has made us understand that
Tommy is " most remarkable like [us]." He has
crept into the native mind, and given the reader not
clever guesses as to the Oriental's point of view, but
actual bits of his psychology. He has made the
outside world know Anglo-Indian society. More
recently he has given us some marvellous studies of
the Jungle-folk. None of these things had ever
been done before.

To some observers Mr. Kipling's treatment of
machinery constitutes the most original feature of
his work. It is true that no writer has with such
persistence and brilliancy sung the " Song o' Steam."
Yet it must not be forgotten that Walt Whitman
celebrated modern mechanical inventions with great
imaginative power. How far the younger writer is
indebted to Whitman may be disputed, but absolute
originality in this field can hardly be conceded to the
author of " McAndrew's Hymn." Did not Whitman, addressing the locomotive, speak of

" Thy black cylindric body, golden brass, and silvery steel,
Thy ponderous side-bars, parallel and connecting rods, gy-
rating, shuttling at thy sides " ? [1]

Was it not Whitman who wrote the finest description of the ocean cable ever penned :

" The seas inlaid with eloquent gentle wires " ? [2]

---

[1] " To a Locomotive in Winter."
[2] " Passage to India."

The two poets are alike in their idealization of machinery. They differ chiefly in this : the younger man knows machinery not only as a poet, but also as an inventor; the older man looked at it with the eyes of a poet only.

But Mr. Kipling is original in manner as well as in theme. In the *Jungle Books* he has created a distinctly new form of literature — as different from Æsop as from his other closest prototype in this kind, Mr. Joel Chandler Harris. He has invented for his short stories a prose style so bare of all conventional and pedantic devices that puzzled critics have denied to him the possession of style at all. He seems to write not in words but in pictures. Still more original, if anything, is his verse. "Kiplingesque manner" has come to stand for a well-known type. Its features are virility, a fondness for specific words, the frequent union of the beautiful with the grotesque, and a swift and splendid metrical movement as inimitable as it is indefinable.

After all it may be doubted whether Mr. Kipling has ever done a more original thing than in making the cockney jargon of the *Barrack Room Ballads* poetic. That the dialect of Burns is suited to purposes of poetry is very plain. It is archaic, not ignorant. The Atkins vernacular, on the other hand, is not properly dialect at all. We should say on general principles that this corrupt patois, this very refuse of human speech, is totally unsuited for the

poet's use, and should incline to doubt whether any
living poet could do more than to make it into witty
verse.   Yet whoever does not call " Mandalay " and
" Danny Deever " poetry is ignorant of poetry when
he sees it.   " To make the common marvellous,
as if it were a revelation, is a test of genius,"
said Mr. Lowell.   No writer of our century has
met this test more unmistakably than Rudyard
Kipling.

16. IMPERIALISM. — Mr. Kipling is the Cecil
Rhodes of literature.   No one has done more to
give Englishmen an imaginative conception of their
colonial possessions, or to cultivate in them a lofty
patriotic pride.   " Mr. Kipling's most characteristic
work is really saturated with politics," says *Blackwood's*, — " the politics of true statesmanship."   It
is difficult to decide whether his influence is greater in
literature or in public affairs.   His voice is for the
closer union of English-speaking peoples, and bitterly
against a false liberalism that would extend the
privileges of self-government in advance of the preparation of subject races to receive it, — equally
against, also, the insular complacency of the " Little
Englander " who is indifferent to the welfare of
colonial dependencies or who selfishly ignores it.
" What should they know of England," Kipling
asks in " The English Flag," " who only England
know ? "   In his great chant of imperialism, " The
Native-Born," he pledges faith

" To the last and the largest Empire,
To the map that is half unrolled.''

There have been laureates of England in plenty, but never before a laureate of the British Empire. Born in India, educated in England, a traveller in South Africa and almost every colony that owes allegiance to Victoria, for several years an American resident, — Mr. Kipling has indeed followed " the war-drum of the white man round the world." [1]

For his intense allegiance to Britain Mr. Kipling has not escaped criticism. A recent writer has complained of his devotion to the idea of " the supremacy of the British Empire over all the globe for the sake of materialism and by means of militarism. . . . The virtue which Kipling lays stress upon is the military virtue of obedience for militant ends." [2] This is a partial misconception. Mr. Kipling is none the less human or representative; on the contrary, he is more so, because so national. A flower shares the general life of nature only by feeding on the soil around its root. No one can become a citizen of the world until he has been truly a citizen of his own country, till he has been able to say with Whitman :

" I stand in my place with my own day here.''

Thus much for the implied charge of provincialism. As for Kipling's materialism, it is plain that the

---

[1] " Song of the Banjo."
[2] Charlotte Porter in *Poet-Lore*.

objector has failed to read between his lines. Mr.
Kipling is not at bottom a materialist, but a psychologist, I had almost said moralist. The material
product resulting from human energy interests him
as the tangible expression of character. As to the
" militant ends," the notion is so patently absurd that
it hardly calls for refutation. That the end he has
in view is material and vulgar prosperity — this is a
gratuitous assumption denied by every line of his
writings. He seeks the permanent well-being of the
world, an end to be achieved only, as he reasons, by
securing the well-being of that race or of those races
best fitted to dominate the world, to shape its ideals,
and to control its destiny. In Mr. Kipling's prose
and verse the goal toward which the Saxon struggle
for supremacy is directed is

> " An hundred times made plain,
> To seek another's profit
> And work another's gain." [1]

One cannot deny, however, that the immediate
means by which Mr. Kipling looks for the advance
of civilization is militarism. It is not the God of
Things as They Should Be that he worships. If
there be any defect in his philosophy of human
progress it lies in his danger of relatively undervalu-
ing the effectiveness of quiet spiritual forces as
opposed to the forces more spectacular and demonstra-
tive. We would respectfully recall to his memory a

---

[1] " The White Man's Burden."

passage from a very old-fashioned book : " And, be-
hold, the Lord passed by, and a great and strong wind
rent the mountains, and brake in pieces the rocks
before the Lord ; but the Lord was not in the wind :
and after the wind an earthquake; but the Lord was
not in the earthquake; and after the earthquake a
fire ; but the Lord was not in the fire : and after the
fire a still small voice."

17. TREATMENT OF NATURE. — In traversing
his imperial domain with Mr. Kipling we are impressed not only with the sense of tramping armies,
rolling ships, and flying flags, we are struck by the
out-of-door feeling of it all, by the great stretches of
plain and ocean and coast-line, and the sound of the
wind about our ears.

Yet nature, in the thought of Mr. Kipling, is
simply the background for humanity.   He has little
of the contemplative spirit.   He has nothing of that
half-indolent, brooding receptiveness of effects from
every source whereby Tennyson permitted a scene
to mirror itself in quiet harmony on his mind's
retina.   He is too impatient, too alert for this.
You would hardly expect to find him writing a song
to the daisy or a sonnet on a daffodil, or celebrating
the joys of solitary communion with the landscape.
Nor has he any " philosophy of nature."   He con-
ceives of nature neither, as Wordsworth and Shelley
do, as if she possessed a distinctly personal life, nor
as Keats does, as though she were peopled with

mythical beings apart both from human life and
her own. He constantly personifies natural phe-
nomena, but never forgets that he is talking in
metaphor. Note several instances of his interpre-
tation of natural scenery or force in terms of
human activity :

> " The wind that tramps the world."
> " The deaf, gray-bearded seas."
> " The hours struck clear in the cabin ; the nosing bows
> slapped and scuffled with the seas."
> " All night the red flame stabbed the sky
> With wavering, wind-tossed spears."
> " Hot moist orchids that make mouths at you."
> " The winter moon was walking the untroubled sea."
> " Driving a whispering wall of water to right and left."
> " The Peace Rock lay across the shallows like a long snake,
> and the little tired ripples hissed as they dried on its hot side."

Personification is common in all imaginative writing, but its use in Kipling deserves special note.
His interest is so exclusively centred in the activi-
ties of men and women that he has to transfer their
various forms of effort to his landscape before entering into its spirit with much sympathy. Thus we
hear of the seawater's " choking and chuckling," of
the winds " herding the purple-blue cloud-shadows,"
of " the kiss of rain," of the earth " breathing lightly
in the pauses between the howling of the jackals,"
of " the thunder chattering overhead," of " the trees
thrashing each other." The advantage of this descriptive method lies in its vividness ; it translates

the less familiar into the more familiar : the abstract
conception into the concrete image.

18. DESCRIPTION. — If he portrays natural scenery with a few vital strokes, Mr. Kipling applies the
same method to all his descriptive passages.   His
great achievement is that of actually making the
reader see things.   What a second-class writer
would dredge the dictionary in describing, he packs
into a curt, truncated sentence.   "Give me one
adjective," he seems to say, "and I will do more
than you could with a portfolio of them ; but you
must let me choose the adjective."   His selective
instinct is unfaltering.   He picks out from · the
myriad details of a scene those two or three which
suggest the whole.   His method is never the patient,
elaborate manner of Tennyson, laying in every line
and shadow with Pre-Raphaelite precision.   Mr.
Kipling spirits you out of doors.   You are not
reading about a place, you are seated square *in* it.
It is nothing less than verbal magic.   Take, for
instance, this picture of his beloved North-country
drawn by a homesick Afridi horse-thief : "The
bloom of the peach-orchards is upon all the Valley,
and *here* is only dust and a great stink.   There is a
pleasant wind among the mulberry-trees, and the
streams are bright with snow-water, and the caravans go up and the caravans go down, and a hundred fires sparkle in the gut of the Pass, and tent-peg
answers hammer-nose, and pack-horse squeals to

pack-horse across the drift smoke of the evening.
It is good in the North now. Come back with me."[1]
There are few situations which Mr. Kipling is
unable to describe with success, but two, at least,
he pictures with a mastery which is beyond anything
in modern literature. Whenever he writes of the
open sea or whenever he touches upon a battle-
scene, he is preëminent. Nowhere, unless in Shakespeare, shall one discover sea-pictures which equal
some of those in " A Matter of Fact " and " *Captains
Courageous.*" None of his contemporaries, unless
Mr. Stephen Crane, and scarcely one of his prede-
cessors, no, not Sir Walter himself, has approached
the vividness of certain battle-pictures in " With
the Main Guard," *The Light that Failed*, " Mutiny
of the Mavericks," and " Drums of the Fore and
Aft." They are painted in blood and fire.

19. CHARACTERIZATION. — If description is Mr.
Kipling's strongest side, character-drawing is his
weakest. Or let us say that with him characterization is another kind of description. His fiction
forms a sort of verbal " biograph " : though his
pictures move, they remain pictures none the less.
After reading his stories one is left with an impression of remarkably vigorous delineation, but not
with the feeling that one has watched the natural
and inevitable growth of character. Hardly anybody, indeed, develops in Kipling. Maisie and

<hr>

[1] " Dray Wara Yow Dee."

Dick, Tarvin and Kate — they are the same at the end of the book as at the outset. Harvey Cheyne suffers a sea-change, perhaps, but his sudden regeneration is not so much a study in the evolution of character as a study in the relation of environment to conduct. Nor is there anything save the different circumstances surrounding them that enables us to tell apart certain of the men and women who reappear in the short stories. Mrs. Hauksbee is not clearly discriminated from Mrs. Polly Mallowe or from Mrs. Harriet Herriott. Mrs. Reiver differs from her hated rival only by being plainly labelled : " wicked in a business-like way," and " not honestly mischievous like Mrs. Hauksbee." Mowgli, marvellous creature though he is, is less an individualized character than a type of the natural man highly idealized. The familiar musketeers may seem to refute the truth of our generalization. But Learoyd, closely as his dialect is caught, is on the whole rather shadowy — an " 'ayrick in trousies ; " Ortheris, while a more clear-cut figure, is a generic cockney ; and Mulvaney a typical son of Erin plus something of Mr. Rudyard Kipling. The Irishman and Londoner are actual, but they fail to live and move and have their being as Lear does, or Hamlet, or Falstaff, or Doctor Primrose, or Colonel Newcome. Verisimilitude is not verity. It must be observed that in the case of all his most striking personages Mr. Kipling has the distinct advantage (in this he is Dickens' own son) of choosing individuals who are marked by some external idiosyncrasy. Mulvaney is at once set apart from the rest by his Irish wit and brogue, by his height, by his appetite for strong waters. Otheris is remembered by his diminutive stature, his dog-stealing propensities, and his fondness for the Adjective. Were the author to choose characters whose appearance and manner was similar, and aim to differentiate them by subtle mental differences which called for powers of insight rather than for exercise of the descriptive faculty, his inferiority to more than one contemporary — take Mr. Meredith as a single example — would be apparent.

Mr. Kipling's characters seem to be infinitely various, yet they are principally limited to the folk who engage in the day's work. With spineless, indolent men who take their ideas from books, with flaccid, washed-out women who can't ride a horse or run a house, he has little sympathy. The few people of this sort who appear in his pages are introduced only to be hastily chastised and dismissed. When he approaches the narrowly evangelical type so concerned with prayers and phylacteries that it is content to leave the day's work to others, his usual tolerance deserts him and he descends into fiercest caricature. When he describes children he is apt to make them monsters of precocity. In order to interest him they must bring things to pass, even like their stalwart fathers and mothers whom he loves. Wee Willie Winkie, a prodigy of six years, effects a marvellous rescue of a young lady surrounded by bandits. Tods, a youth of the same age, discusses politics with Indian officials and actually influences legislation. What a spectacle is this! Men at work, women at work, children at work! And behind the ranks of toiling and fighting humanity the imperturbable young poet urging them on by word and example to still greater activity!

But Mr. Kipling's characterization is not only varied and strenuous, it is saturated with humor. The grim sardonic wit of the early ballads, the irony of the early stories, melt gradually into a kinder spirit — but the fun is still there. It is often mingled so closely with pathos that they cannot easily be disentangled. "Comic stuff and tragic sadness" stand cheek by jowl in "Thrown Away;" in "Tomlinson" we laugh and shudder at the same moment.

   "Vulgar tunes that bring the laugh that brings the groan —
   I can rip your very heart-strings out with those,"

boasts the poet's banjo. Only writers of extraordinary power can touch at the same instant the springs of merriment and of tears. Shakespeare, of course, is the master in this sort, but Mr. Kipling is an apt disciple.

I have already said, however, that character-drawing is not Mr. Kipling's forte. He finds it difficult to keep his own personality out of that of his creation, and is always in danger of introducing false touches into his very best work. In "With the Main Guard," after Ortheris has produced his bottles of gingerade, Mulvaney inquires, "Where did ye get ut, ye Machiavel?" Again, take this: "Ortheris had considered the question in all its bearings. He spoke, chewing his pipe-stem meditatively the while :

> " ' " Go forth, return in glory,
>   To Clusium's royal 'ome :
>   An' round these bloomin' temples 'ang
>   The bloomin' shields o' Rome." ' " [1]

Once more (Mulvaney is speaking) : " Spit it out, Jock, an' bellow melojus to the moon. It takes an earthquake or a bullet graze to fetch aught out av you. Discourse, Don Juan! The a-moors av Lotharius Learoyd!" [2]

Bessie, illiterate and immoral, thus solicits Torpenhow in *The Light that Failed :* " Oh, please, 'tisn't as if I was asking you to marry me. I wouldn't think of it. But cou— couldn't you take and live with me till Miss Right comes along? I'm only Miss Wrong, I know, but I'd work my hands to the bare bone for you." Another singularly infelicitous touch is that where our author makes the

---

[1] " The Incarnation of Krishna Mulvaney."
[2] " On Greenhow Hill."

" Brushwood girl," most sensitive and highly-bred of women, exclaim in a moment of strong feeling, " My God ! " One unfortunate line in " Gunga Din " mars a masterpiece. Even Mr. Kipling fails to convince us that a water-carrier who is dying of a mortal wound, model of unselfishness though he be, would gasp with his last death-rattle : " I 'ope you liked your drink." It is precisely what he would not have said.

20. MASTERY OF THE SHORT STORY. — Mr. Kipling has inexhaustible inventiveness. To have written more than one hundred and fifty stories, hardly one of which gives the reader the impression of being some familiar set of incidents turned up again, is to have revealed very unusual talents, but to have handled these plots with such sure artistic sense is to have accomplished far more.

Possibly the most wonderful feat that Kipling has performed is the mastery of the short story as a literary form. In accomplishing this he has succeeded where nearly every English writer who preceded him has failed. Englishmen have been able to write a good three-volume novel ever since Richardson, but, with perhaps half a dozen exceptions, they have not produced a single short story that can take its place beside the little perfections of France and America. Yet Mr. Kipling has written more than a score, to be very conservative, that are masterly in form and brilliant in content. They are not pages torn from some unfinished novel, they " are cast at once, as if in a mold."

Even in the *Plain Tales* this unique power is apparent. These early stories were marred by mannerisms which the author has since discarded. Yet note that these very mannerisms were always employed in the interest of conciseness. He abbreviates almost to the point of obscurity; he ends a broken sentence with a dash; he omits his finite verbs; he overwhelms the lay reader with a flood of military initials, since you see it saves space to write C. O. rather than commanding officer. Even his trick of saying, " But that is another story . . . ," shows his conscious, if not ostentatious, effort to keep himself within bounds. The result is a sort of tale condensed almost to anecdote. Introductions and preliminary explanations are suggested by a phrase or cut out; conclusions exist in your stimulated imagination, you will not find them on the page; not a word anywhere could be spared or added. The power of the tales is in their suddenness. They are not paintings, growing, stroke by stroke, under the artist's brush. They are stereopticon pictures projected instantly upon the screen.

In some of his recent fiction Mr. Kipling, while showing gain in analysis and maturity of thought, gives evidence of having lost this early power. He has seldom been at his best in the elaborate method.

Maisie, in *The Light that Failed*, who is described at length, is less real to our imagination that the red-haired girl, revealed in three or four lightning glimpses. It is the misfortune of Mr. Kipling's later style that he is explicit where he was once suggestive. In such tales as " The Devil and the Deep Sea " and "The Ship that Found Herself " he shows that he has forgotten the force of the epigram : " The secret of being dull is to tell all you know."

It may be said in passing that the swift concise-ness which seems to have departed from his prose style has been, oddly enough, transferred to his poetry. His recent ballads are so tightly packed with meaning that their rapid allusiveness often approaches the verge of obscurity.

21. MASTERY OF METRE. — Yet it must be said that, on the whole, Mr. Kipling's mastery of form in poetical composition is no less remarkable than his mastery of form in story-writing. His metres are as various as his themes. Though his favorite metrical scheme is simple, his inventiveness, when he leaves his swinging ballad measures, and sets out in quest of variety, is almost unrivalled. No matter how intricate the problem he sets himself, he is certain to solve it. "The Song of the Banjo" is an instance in point. It presents technical diffi-culties that would have baffled any other living writer, yet the poet overrides them with ingenuity and apparent ease.

It may be questioned, however, whether the music inherent in Mr. Kipling's lines has much subtlety, or in any sense equals his force, metrical facility, or precision of phrase. So many of his poems are heel-and-toe choruses that one doubts whether the poet will ever wholly emancipate himself from this regimental mood. " White Horses " and a few other lyrics begin to give us hope, but it must be said in general that he marches in strict time to the band. What he gains in speed, he loses in repose; what he gains in ornament of phrase, he loses in simplicity. Mr. Kipling's verse is rhetorical and declamatory. Very little of it can be classed with that highest order of poetry, devoid of every suspicion of " style," which Nature seems to have penned herself. Representative examples in this kind are Wordsworth's Lucy lyrics and the best songs of Burns and of Blake. Brilliant is not the word one applies to these. One never thinks of the authors as composing them. They are inevitable. Mr. Kipling's poetry, on the other hand, is more like that of Byron, of Campbell, of Dryden, of Macaulay, though far surpassing in one respect or another the work of each of them. It is excessively clever, it is eloquent and sonorous to a degree, but it falls short of that " nobly plain manner" admired by Matthew Arnold, which is really the crowning triumph of expression. The one immortal exception is the " Recessional," which is as unadorned as a Greek statue. For once feeling and expression absolutely fuse; there is no suspicion of artifice. See how it depends on nouns and verbs :

> "The tumult and the shouting dies —
> The captains and the kings depart."

In the first seven lines there are only two descriptive adjectives.

22. DICTION. — Mr. Kipling has the gift of the inevitable word. " It is the paradox of poetry that it permits no synonyms." Like every true poet, he is not content with an excellent epithet, he must have the absolute one. It is in this power that his success as a poet preëminently, and as a prose writer, very largely, lies. Let him take a jog-trot metre, such as that of " The White Man's Burden " (see what doggerel his host of imitators have made out of it), and then watch what he can accomplish. Does not his triumph consist principally in the glove-like fit of such phrases as " new-caught sullen peoples, half devil and half child " ? The commonplace tramp of " McAndrew's Hymn " is saved from utter monotony by such lines as this : " By night those soft, lasceevious stars leered from those velvet skies."

In his choice of words Mr. Kipling always strikes for concreteness. His aversion to the indefinite and abstract amounts almost to horror. Circumlocutions and euphemisms he spews out of his mouth. Not only does he call a spade a spade, he refuses to supplant honest old Saxon words, which were good enough for Bible translators and for Shakespeare, with those roundabout equivalents which a sophisticated modern taste regards more delicate. His passion for specific words has betrayed him, also, into a curious literary fallacy. A specific word presents a more lively image than a general or class term; hence, he argues, the precise word which a tradesman or mechanic employs has more vividness than an indefinite term applied by the layman. Consistent with his theory, he dumps into a few of his later stories the whole vocabulary of technical cant, forgetting that even a general term which we understand presents to the eye a clearer image than a technical term at whose meaning we can only guess. On the whole, Mr. Kipling writes the clearest and most picturesque prose of any living author. His use of technical jargon is at the worst a mistaken essay in a right direction, and as yet appears to be rather a dangerous tendency than a settled fault. We would remind him, however, of the words he once wrote of Wressley : " He began his book in the land he was writing of. . . . He must have guessed that he needed the white light of local color on his palette. This is a dangerous paint for amateurs to play with." Yes, Mr. Kipling, and it is dangerous paint even for accomplished artists. A few nautical terms or names of tools and machines add reality to a description, but a solid page of this sort of thing is apt to be a bore. When one has been treated to whole paragraphs reeking with information about garboard-strakes, link-heads, crank-throws, crates, and fall-ropes, one may be pardoned for exclaiming, even if one has the devil for company, " It's clever, but is it art?" To the mind of the present writer there can be only one answer.

But Mr. Kipling seeks not only for the most concrete, but also for the most suggestive word. When he says he had " the smell of the *drinking* earth in [his] nostrils," he chooses an epithet that connotes the whole impression. When he says of Kaa, the huge python, that " he seemed to *pour* himself along the ground," and of Mulvaney, when he returned from his Incarnation, that he " disappeared to the waist in a *wave* of joyous dogs," he attains the same sort of magic. In his effort to cast imaginative spells, he makes use of imitative words, frequently invented by himself.

> " And out of the grass on a sudden broke
> A spirtle of fire, a whorl of smoke."

> " Then Tomlinson he gripped the bars and yammered, ' Let me in.' "

> " There was a row in Silver street — an' I was in it too ;
> We passed the time o' day, an' then the belts went whir-raru."

> " There was a profusion of squabby, pluffy cushions."

> " The swords whinny-whicker like angry kites."

> " Elephints a-pilin' teak
> In the sludgy, squdgy creek."

" Forty-pounder guns:
Jiggery-jolty to and fro."
" I did not want to plowter about any more in the drizzle
and the dark."

These words are invariably apt. If there is no
such noun as " bobble " nor such verb as " plopped,"
one feels there ought to be, and that Mr. Kipling
does right to introduce them. Equally descriptive
are his words which stand for repeated sounds : " bat-
bat-bat," " tap-tap-tapped," " sip-sip-sipping," " wop-
wop-wop," and any number of others. But perhaps the most daring of his inventions are the words
imitating characteristic sounds made by animals, as
" Aurgh " (tiger), " Hrrump " (elephant), " Kssha "
and " Ngssh " (snake), " Ya-la-hi ! Yalaha ! " (wolf),
" chitter-chatter " (leaping rat), " chug-drug " (boar
sharpening his tusks on a bole). Nor does Kipling's
coinage of words stop with the class where sound
connotes sense. He improvises on whatever instrument he plays. Is he after humorous effect ?
He out-Brownings Browning with such monstrosi-
ties as scarabeousness, adjutaunter, special-cor-
respondently and whalesome, or such compound
adjectives as expensive-pictures-of-the-nude-adorned,
Seidlitz-powders-colored, Government-broad-arrow-
shaped, and hair-trunk-thrown-in-the-trade. He
forms one part of speech out of another, or gives
an existing word a new ending, or restores obsolete
forms at his pleasure : badling, thumbling, empties

(noun), grown-ups, high-grassed, hogged, horsehood, know-how (noun), long-ago (adjective), old-maidism, pine-needled, rocketed, smashment, Sahibdom, vagabonded, springily, bad-worded (verb), brassily, gentled (verb), gridironing, piglet, deerlets, rabbity, tailing (part.) brotherliwise. His compound words are innumerable. Fire-fanged, knotty-rooted, over-ankle, rain-channelled, sweetish-sourish, scissor-legged, twiney-tough — these are samples out of a list numbering several hundred which I have collected from his prose.

23. FIGURATIVE LANGUAGE. — Mr. Kipling shows his selective instinct no less in his choice of figures than in that of words. He is one of the greatest masters of metaphor since Shakespeare.

It may almost be said that Mr. Kipling writes in nothing except figures. What is the whole body of his recent work but metaphor? A writer of less penetration might have inveighed against the materialism of an age like ours. Mr. Kipling idealizes it, lifts it all into the region of symbol. Every crank and piston is a letter in his alphabet of spiritual power. He is the great allegorist of modern times.

Metaphors, using the word in the rhetorical sense, are employed frequently in Kipling, yet so discriminately, and with such an insistent originality, as always to avoid the merely florid. His tropes are notable equally for a quaint unconventionality and for aptness.

So remarkable is Mr. Kipling's use of metaphor that it deserves extensive illustration. A single figure of speech, however, may be taken as typical. Note the directness of the following similes : After a river flood, which swept all barriers before it, " the piers of the Barhwi Bridge showed like broken teeth in the jaw of an old man."[1] " The grass-stems held the heat exactly as boiler-tubes do."[2] " The lightning spattered the sky as a thrown egg spatters a barn-door."[3] " Little by little, very softly and pleasantly, she began taking the conceit out of Pluffles, as they take the ribs out of an umbrella before recovering it."[4] "The Colonel's face set like the Day of Judgment framed in gray bristles."[5] " Dick delivered himself of the saga of his own doings, with all the arrogance of a young man speaking to a woman. From the beginning he told the tale, the I— I— I's flashing through the records as telegraph-poles fly past the traveller."[6]

Kipling frequently introduces a sort of Homeric simile which suggests the influence of the *Iliad* and *Odyssey* so strikingly that it is difficult to believe he

[1] " In Flood Time."
[2] " Bubbling Well Road."
[3] " The Return of Imray."
[4] " The Rescue of Pluffles."
[5] "His Wedded Wife."
[6] *The Light that Failed.*

lacks intimate acquaintance with them.   Here is an example from *The Naulahka :* " His eyes were red with opium, and he walked as a bear walks when he is overtaken by the dawn in a poppy-field, where he has gorged his fill through the night watches." *The Light that Failed* yields good examples : " As swiftly as a reach of still water is crisped by the wind, the rock-strewn ridges and scrub-topped hills were troubled and alive with armed men."   Again : " The mind was quickened, and the revolving thoughts ground against each other as mill-stones grind when there is no corn between."   Once more : " A refrain, slow as the clacking of a capstan when the boat comes unwillingly up to the bars where the men sweat and tramp in the shingle." [1]

24. PROSE STYLE IN GENERAL. — Mr. Kipling's style, in a very remarkable degree, reflects his personality.   His words do not conceal, they reveal him.   What Whitman wrote regarding *Leaves of Grass* applies to the works of Kipling :

> " This is no book,
> Who touches this touches a man."

The impression of really holding conversation with the author is due in part to his honesty and earnestness.   It is attributable quite as much to the style itself.   The construction is that of speech. Kipling never " reads like a book."   He employs

---

[1] See *Athenæum*, April 18, 1891.

the tongue in which we buy and sell, and make love, and confess our sins. His sentences are brief and idiomatic; the order of the words is seldom inverted; there are few parenthetical clauses; the words themselves are usually short and prevailingly Saxon.

An involved style is generally an obscure style. Kipling's clearness is due partly to his natural and effective arrangement of words; partly also to his unerring choice of the word that fits.

His style has movement as well as clearness. It sweeps one on with great swiftness to the story's climax. There is no halting by the wayside to pluck an epigram. Mr. Kipling sees his work too much as a whole, he is too jealous for the integrity of his central impression, to distract the reader with · aphorisms. Perhaps, too, he considers the epigrammatic style to savor of pedantry, as witness the following quotation from one of the *Plain Tales:* "'No wise man has a policy,' said the Viceroy. 'A policy is the blackmail levied on the Fool by the Unforeseen. I am not the former, and I do not believe in the latter.' I do not quite see what this means, unless it refers to an insurance policy. Perhaps it was the Viceroy's way of saying, 'Lie low.'"[1]

Regarding the force of Kipling's style, I have already spoken. Force, next to sincerity, is its prevailing note. Concentration, crispness, realism, coherence, suggestiveness, all these, too, are part of our

---

[1] "A Germ Destroyer."

author's equipment. But it is often pointed out that he has the defects of his qualities. His virility, we are told, sometimes descends into coarseness, his realistic manner into slang, his swift " go " into jerkiness and journalese. He is always powerful, he is not always highly-bred. In his passion for clearness and force he sometimes forgets how many other qualities go to make up a finished style. The subtle rhythmical movement, the cadence, the pervasive overtones which mark much of De Quincey's prose, and Cardinal Newman's, and Louis Stevenson's, these, for the most part, are absent from the author's page.

But it may be said in Kipling's defence that the sort of verbal incantation which imparts almost a sensuous thrill to the reader, perhaps seems to him essentially insincere. It also may be said that a highly beautified style is excluded by his persistent aim to make his writings as much like spoken speech as he can. That he is able, moreover, when it suits his purpose, to write paragraphs where rhythm is a marked feature, is shown in not a few stories, especially in narratives put into the mouths of natives, and in several of the Jungle tales.

Kipling's style, however, needs no apology. His art is perfect if it perfectly achieve its purpose ; we never should pronounce an author's method defective till we have inquired what he aims to do. Mr. Kipling occasionally shocks us with his coarseness. But perhaps we need to be shocked. Granted that

he violates our conventions.   It does us good to
reëxamine the ground for these conventions.   Let
us admit that he is deficient in rhythm.   Rhythm is
what we ask for in a lullaby, not in a battle-slogan
or an alarm of fire.   The man who strives to shake
you out of your self-satisfaction, and to nerve you
for conflict or danger, ought hardly to be quarrelled
with because he refuses to sing you to sleep.   Kipling's message is not for the ear, but for the emotions and the will.

Of course this peremptory, challenging style is
not universally popular.   He or she — more often
she — whose ideal of literature is completely met by
the elaborately polite while beautiful style of Ad-
dison, whose taste is unpleasantly disturbed by Swift
and wholly outraged by Carlyle, — such a reader
will certainly shrink from the brusqueness of these
" straight-flung words and few."   Kipling's style is
not custom-made.   Like Whitman, he has "gone
freely with powerful uneducated persons."   Readers
who look for evening clothes and court bows — who
care less for literary manner than for literary manners — will cut his acquaintance just as soon as he
ceases to be a fashionable fad.

25. INFLUENCE. — Is Mr. Kipling a classic?
Who knows, or cares?   His fate will probably be
the common one :

> " Some of him lived, but the most of him died
> (Even as you and I !) "

The permanency of his fame is doubtless Mr. Kipling's least concern. Is it not the third-rate poet who sighs with Cowley:

"What shall I do to be forever known
And make the age to come my own"?

Time takes fine revenges on all such.

But whether or not Mr. Kipling is a classic, it cannot be disputed that he is a force. The man who has created a new respect for poetry, who has conquered a new class of readers, who is already quoted, imitated, parodied in every English-speaking land, who, while still in his early thirties, influences the policy of nations and marks time for their marching feet, who gathers the civilized world at his bedside to pray for his recovery, — surely this man is something far greater than the occupant of a literary pedestal — he is the leader and friend of our common race.

26. SUMMARY. — I have attempted to show in this chapter on what grounds Mr. Kipling's work may properly be called great; I have attempted to trace the development of his dramatic genius through three stages which I have ventured to call the satiric, the sympathetic, and the spiritual; and I have finally discussed a number of his general characteristics in detail. In so short a treatise it can hardly be hoped that anything more than an intelligent outline has been furnished the student, yet the writer trusts a few things have been made clear:

1. Mr. Kipling is the most prominent figure in the world of letters, and has made the most rapid of modern literary reputations.

2. He has conquered three classes : the literary class who read for style; the average reader who reads for amusement ; the non-reading class who are fascinated by his familiarity with their material world of commerce, trade, and machinery.

3. He is a great political force.

4. His work is notable for power, originality, range, health, and sincerity.

5. Nature is to him simply the background for the play of strenuous human emotions.

6. His philosophy of life is marked by vigor and optimism.

7. His temper is distinctly masculine. He is always strong, and sometimes coarse.

8. His manner is realistic ; his aim idealistic.

9. His forte is description, and he is a master of language.

10. His characterization is not always good, and is never of the highest kind.

11. His ability to invent plots seems exhaustless, and his mastery of the short-story form is unrivalled in contemporary literature. He has not, however, been especially successful in writing novels.

12. His verse is brilliant and rhetorical, and has at least once attained the " nobly plain manner " of the highest poetry.

CHAPTER THREE

AMERICAN, AN. (*The Seven Seas.*) — This description of the typical American contains much wholesome criticism.   While it aims to be just, it is hardly calculated to flatter national vanity.   It is in part a parody on Emerson's *Brahma*, but it is much longer than the earlier poem. A sample of its quality may be had from the next to the last of its fourteen stanzas :

> " Enslaved, illogical, elate,
>   He greets th' embarrassed Gods, nor fears
> To shake the iron hand of Fate
>   Or match with Destiny for beers."

> " To me it gives a sense of his penetration and his grasp that nothing else does.   I am tempted to call the piece the most important thing, intellectually, in Mr. Kipling's new volume of *The Seven Seas.*" — *W. D. Howells.*

AMERICAN NOTES. — This series of letters contributed to a newspaper in India (the *Pioneer*, Allahabad), was the result of Mr. Kipling's American tour of 1889. Their publication in book form by a New York house (1891) was unauthorized.   They are satiric pictures of society in the United States.   Marred by journalistic smartness and superficiality and by very evident prejudice against America, but entertaining and clever.   (See the American *Bookman* for April, 1898.)

The complete series of letters of which these are a part were published in the *Pioneer* under the title *From Sea to Sea*, and have this year (1899) been republished in book form under the original title by Mr. Kipling's authorized publishers, Doubleday & McClure Company. (See *From Sea to Sea*.)

AMIR'S HOMILY, THE. (*Life's Handicap*.) — A thief, brought to trial before the Amir, avers that he stole because he was starving, having been unable to find work. The despot tells him that he lies, "since any man who will, may find work and daily bread." The magistrate then relates a tale of his "evil days," when he himself was starving. He refused gifts, asking only for work. He was finally successful. Day after day he wrought as a coolie on a daily wage of four annas. Then turning to the prisoner he commands that he be led away to execution.

AMONG THE RAILWAY FOLK. (See *From Sea to Sea*.)

ANCHOR SONG. (*The Seven Seas*.) — A sailor-song first published as Envoy to *Many Inventions*, and subsequently included in *The Seven Seas*. It has a rhythmical movement, but fairly bristles with nautical terms.

"A magnificent bit of long-syllable versification." — *Academy*.

ANGUTIVUN TINA. — A poem following "Quiquern" in the *Second Jungle Book*. It is supposedly a free translation of the "Song of the Returning Hunter," as the Esquimaux sang it after seal-spearing.

ANSWER, AN. (*Ballads*.) — The truth that grief and apparent failure are justified if they form part of God's purpose is taught in this parable of a rose, who, tattered and stem-broken, complains to God, and receives an answer which comforts her as she bows her head to die.

ARREST OF LIEUTENANT GOLIGHTLY, THE. (*Plain Tales.*) — The story of a vain man's humiliation. Golightly, dressed fastidiously, is caught in a tremendous rainstorm which reduces his new white helmet to dough, covers his gaiters with mud, and causes the dye-stuffs of suit, tie, and hat-lining to run. He is mistaken for a deserter for whom the police are looking, and is delivered over to the authorities. After some travelling about in custody, and much struggling and profanity, he is rescued by one of his majors who recognizes the dandy officer under the outward appearance of a dirty tramp.

AT HOWLI THANA. (*In Black and White.*) — The native who relates the tale has been dismissed from the Police for a piece of rascality, and now begs the Sahib to take him into his employ as a messenger. The demand for an explanation of his conduct leads to a willing admission of the facts, but the most nonchalant and ingenious vindication of his motive. The sketch gives us much insight into the strange workings of the Oriental mind.

AT THE END OF THE PASSAGE. (*Life's Handicap.*) — The health of a young assistant engineer at a lonely Indian station is shattered during the hot season by sleeplessness and pure terror, the latter resulting from phantoms created by his feverish and disordered brain. The doctor offers him a testimonial which will secure him leave of absence. He refuses, since the man that would be sent to take his place lacks the physique to endure the Plains, and would, moreover, bring with him his delicate wife now convalescing in Simla. The doomed man, therefore, remains and dies at his post.

AT THE PIT'S MOUTH. (*Under the Deodars.*) — The

place is Simla. The three characters are known as "A
Man and his Wife and a Tertium Quid." The man is in
the Plains "earning money for his wife to spend on
dresses," and writing her daily. The wife is carrying on
a violent flirtation with the Tertium Quid. The affair has
reached almost the point of scandal when it is interrupted
by a tragedy. The two are riding on the Himalayan-
Thibet road, which in places is not over six feet wide,
with a sheer drop into the valley below of between one
thousand and two thousand feet, when the man's mare
shies at a log of wood, and, sinking in the earth loosened
by the heavy rains, falls with her rider to the valley below.

> "When he [Kipling] deals in natural horror (take
> 'At the Pit's Mouth' as a sample, or 'The Other
> Man'), I often find him a master." — *Francis Adams
> in Fortnightly.*

AT TWENTY–TWO. (*In Black and White.*) — An old,
blind miner has married a pretty young wife who carries on
a shameless intrigue with a collier working in the same
gang with her husband. A heavy flood, during the Rains,
breaks through the crust of earth over one of the workings
and pours into the main galleries. The blind man's marvellous knowledge of the mine, born of thirty years' experience, enables him to rescue his own gang and two
others. Among the saved is his wife's paramour. The
latter repays him by eloping with the woman.

> "For skilful presentment in a few bold strokes of a
> strange and moving scene, it would be hard to beat the
> escape from the flooded mine in 'At Twenty-two,' or
> the fanatical riot of 'On the City Wall.' The former
> story, indeed, is a gem of the first water." — *Athe-
> næum.*

BAA, BAA, BLACK SHEEP. (*Wee Willie Winkie.*) — Two children of Anglo-Indian parents are committed to the care of an aunt in England. The latter is an unlovely woman, who has some affection for the little girl, but hates the boy, Punch, and subjects him to a series of petty tortures professedly designed for the good of his soul. His childish exaggerations pronounced to be lies, he is finally forced to actual deception in self-defence, and becomes sullen and suspicious. After five years the parents come to claim their children, discover the barbarous treatment the Black Sheep has received at the hands of Aunty Rosa, and, after some difficulty, win back the good there is in the boy's nature by love and tact.

> " A strange compound of work at first and second hand. . . . But Punch lives with an intense vitality, and here, without any indiscretion, we may be sure that Mr. Kipling has looked inside his own heart and drawn from memory." — *Gosse.*

BACK TO THE ARMY AGAIN. (*The Seven Seas.*) — A British soldier who has seen several years' service returns after a time to the army, professing to be as ignorant of things military as any new recruit, but he fails to deceive the sergeant. It is evident from his song that he takes pleasure in coming back, and pride in the prospect of "learnin' the others their trade."

BALLAD OF BOH DA THONE, THE. (*Ballads.*) — A gruesome story of an outlaw chief unsuccessfully hunted down by an Irish company in the "Black Tyrone." The captain marries and settles down, for the time-being forgetful of his quest. Meanwhile a native servant slays the Boh and sends his head by mail to the captain. The latter opens the package at breakfast, and the hideous Thing

rolls out on the table. The bride faints. A little Irish
Kathleen, born shortly afterward, bears the Boh's head as
a birthmark.

BALLAD OF EAST AND WEST, THE. (*Ballads.*) — A
story of magnanimity to a fallen foe, and of the appreciation
of bravery even among enemies:

> "There is neither East nor West, Border nor Breed, nor
> Birth,
> When two strong men stand face to face, tho' they come
> from the ends of the earth."

> "One of the greatest pieces of epic narrative which is
> to be found in our literature." — *Saturday Review.*
> "Mr. Kipling's poetical masterpiece." — *Critic,*
> 1892.
> "Worthy to stand by the border ballads of Sir
> Walter Scott." — *Spectator.*
> "A thing to stir the blood like a trumpet." —
> *Academy.*

BALLAD OF THE "BOLIVAR," THE. (*Ballads.*) — A
triumphant song of seven drunken English sailors who had
brought their half-wrecked vessel through a terrific storm
"safe across the bay."

BALLAD OF THE "CLAMPHERDOWN," THE. (*Ballads.*)
— The "Clampherdown," an English war-ship, engages
with a hostile cruiser, and is badly disabled, but when the
enemy demands the captain's sword, he refuses to surrender,
and, being then at close quarters, commands that the cruiser
be boarded. The latter is cleared from end to end, and,
while the war-ship sinks, her crew stands out "to sweep
the sea" on the captured vessel.

BALLAD OF THE KING'S JEST, THE. (*Ballads.*) —

Unsought counsel is not welcome at court. A gossiping youth wins an Oriental king's anger by warning him of the reported advance of the Russians, and is placed in a tree to await and give word of their coming. He is kept there, guarded by bayonets, till he dies of starvation and madness.

> "The inimitable ballad of the 'King's Jest.'" — *Saturday Review.*

BALLAD OF THE KING'S MERCY, THE. (*Ballads.*) — A story of an Oriental despot's arbitrary and cruel conduct, which his court flatterers professed to regard merciful.

BANK FRAUD, A. (*Plain Tales.*) — The manager of an Indian bank has for accountant a conceited and peevish fellow who finally breaks down with consumption. The directors appoint a successor, but the manager, seeing the necessity for keeping up the spirits of his employé 'if he would prolong his life, not only cares for him and uncomplainingly receives his ungrateful fault-finding, but invents a series of letters from the directors, praising the sick man's work and promising increased pay. The invalid's salary is regularly paid him from the manager's own pocket, but the man dies at last in the presence of his benefactor.

BELL—BUOY, THE. — A poem of nine stanzas in *McClure's*, February, 1897. This highly imaginative song is given us in the supposed words of the bell-buoy.

BELTS. (*Ballads.*) — The story of a Dublin street row between an Irish regiment and a body of English cavalry which had a tragic ending.

> "We went away like beaten dogs, an' down the street we bore him,
> The poor dumb corpse that couldn't tell the bhoys were sorry for him."

BERTRAN AND BIMI. (*Life's Handicap.*) — Hans Breitmann, the German orchid collector who tells also the tale of Reingelder (*q.v.*), relates the story. Bertran is a French naturalist and Bimi his pet orang-outang. Bertran, who has had Bimi twelve years, marries. The beast is jealous of the woman and kills her. Bertran, in return, kills the orang-outang, but in the unequal struggle is himself slain.

" The horrible story of ' Bertran and Bimi,' though its power cannot be denied, is a kind of thing that ought never to have been written. . . . This is nightmare literature." — *Edinburgh Review.*

" ' Bertran and Bimi ' is detestable, and is not in the least saved by being extremely cleverly written." — *Spectator.*

BEYOND THE PALE. (*Plain Tales.*) — Every man should keep to his own caste. Trejago, an Englishman, didn't, and his love intrigue with Bisesa, a pretty Hindu widow of fifteen, resulted only in sorrow to himself and to her. When the affair was discovered by her relatives, barbarous punishment was inflicted on Bisesa, and the man himself was wounded. Thenceforth the girl was lost to him completely.

BIG DRUNK DRAF', THE. (*Soldiers Three.*) — The " big drunk draf' " were the " scourin's an' rinsin's an' Divil's lavin's av the Ould Rig'mint," who were " knockin' red cinders out av ivrything an' ivrybody." The " little orf'cer bhoy " who commanded them was unequal to the situation until Mulvaney, who tells the story, gave him counsel and active assistance in restoring order. The ring-leaders in the disturbance were " pegged out," and the rest of the men driven to their tents. From that day the " little orf'cer bhoy " had his men in complete control.

BILL 'AWKINS. (*The Seven Seas.*) — Tommy wants to find Bill 'Awkins and settle with him for having taken his girl out walking, but when he meets the man he suddenly changes his mind.

"BIRDS OF PREY" MARCH. (*The Seven Seas.*) — The Tommy who sings this song on departing for the front seems to have little hope of returning. He reminds us that

"The jackal an' the kite
'Ave an 'ealthy appetite,"

though he gives a hearty cheer on top of the information.

BISARA OF POOREE, THE. (*Plain Tales.*) — The Bisara of Pooree is a love-charm which, if stolen, possesses potent influence for good. A man steals it and then obtains the consent of a woman, vastly his superior, whom he has long wished to marry, but who has before repelled his advances. The charm is stolen from him in turn, and his fiancée at once suffers a revulsion of feeling and dismisses him.

BITTERS NEAT. (Added to *Plain Tales from the Hills* in the *Outward Bound* edition.) — A girl falls in love with an excellent but dull fellow who, engrossed in his business and unaccustomed to observe women, fails to see it. She refuses meanwhile, greatly to her aunt's anger, a much more "eligible" man. The girl's pitiful little secret gets out, and, sensitive to the gossip around her, she leaves India and returns to England.

BLACK JACK. (*Soldiers Three.*) — A gang of soldiers who conspire to kill an unpopular officer with Mulvaney's rifle and then make it appear that the owner committed the crime are outwitted by the Irishman, who has chanced to overhear the whole plot. He finds the rifle loaded and ready. "I was hot wid rage against thim all, an' I worried the bullet out wid my teeth as fast as I cud, the room bein' empty. Then I tuk my boot an' the clanin'-rod and knocked out the pin av the fallin'-block." The sequel shows how the officer was saved, the man on whom the lot had fallen to do the shooting was himself wounded, Mulvaney vindicated, and poetic justice dealt out generally.

BREAD UPON THE WATERS. (*Day's Work.*) — McPhee, Scotch engineer of the "Breslau," was discharged after twenty years' service for refusing to risk the vessel on a new timing. A rival steamship line gave him employment on the "Kite," a tramp freighter. The "Breslau" soon after broke down when on a voyage, and was towed to port. Thenceforth her management were for retrenchment. Their economy extended to risking a trip on the "Grotkau," a badly-built freighter with a seven-inch crack on the tail-shaft. The "Kite" followed, creeping up by night and falling away by day, until the "Grotkau" was seen signalling for help. A passing liner rescued her crew, but, being a Government mail steamer, was forbidden to tow. How through McPhee's ingenuity and daring this fortune fell to the "Kite," and how the Scotchman received enough of the money-reward to make him wealthy, is related by the hero of the tale himself, and loses nothing in the recital.

BRIDGE–BUILDERS, THE. (*Day's Work.*)—The romance of a flood. Findlayson, of the Public Works Department, had for three years been engaged in constructing a huge bridge over the Ganges. When the work was within a few months of completion, "Mother Gunga" rose in flood, as if angry at this man's outrage upon her, and all but swept the structure away. The engineer refused to leave his post or to eat food. As a preventive against fever he consented to take the opium pills thrust upon him by his native servant, but, unused to the drug, was thrown into a wild dream, in which the gods of India conversed. Gunga's prayer for vengeance on the bridge-builders is denied by Krishna : "They all come to thee at the last. What need to slay them now ? Have pity, mother, for a little, — and it is only for a little."

"'The Bridge-Builders' has in its conception and realization astonishing affinities with Zola. The bridge dominates the narrative in symbolic grandeur, the swarming lives and the accumulated material ever finding metamorphosis in the growth of the monster structure. The dramatic concentration is perfect. . . . The swiftness imparted is unsurpassable." — *L'. Zangwill* (*Cosmopolitan*, 1899).

"The spanning of the Ganges is not merely an engineering achievement : it stands for a type of the losing battle which the old gods of the East fight against new and spiritual forces."— *Macmillan's Magazine.*

"'The Bridge-Builders' will, if we are not greatly mistaken, rank among the masterpieces of this generation."— *Spectator.*

BROKEN–LINK HANDICAP, THE. (*Plain Tales.*) — Kipling reveals in this story as intimate a knowledge of horse-racing as he shows of polo in "The Maltese Cat." At the Chedputter races, the famous Shackles, heretofore invincible, is beaten, through a clever trick played upon Brunt, the little Australian jockey. The way in which the riding-boy's nerve is shaken and the race lost is told with much originality and spirit.

BRONCKHORST DIVORCE–CASE, THE. (*Plain Tales.*)

— Bronckhorst treated his wife like a brute.   His crowning insult was his institution of proceedings on the criminal
count against one Biel, who had been somewhat attentive
to Mrs. Bronckhorst.   It was Strickland (see " Miss Youghal's Sais ") who · discovered that the plaintiff had fabri-
cated false evidence and who made this fact apparent to the
court.   After being acquitted, Biel cut Bronckhorst into
ribbons with a whip.   But his wife wept over him and
nursed him back to life again.

BRUGGLESMITH.   (*Many Inventions.*) — Describes the
author's unpleasant relations with a drunken rascal whom
he calls Brugglesmith — this name being the man's pro-
nunciation of Brook Green, Hammersmith, which he gives
as his address.   A wild night of police courts, ambulances,
officers, narrow escapes from drowning, and a thousand
shifts whereby the young man in evening clothes tries to
rid himself of his effusive companion, but to no purpose,
unite to make up a broadly comic if not farcical story.

" Represents the low-water mark of his genius." —
Prof. Harry Thurston Peck, in Bookman.
" It is amazing to find in this volume such stuff as
' Brugglesmith.' " — *Academy,* 1893.

BRUSHWOOD BOY, THE.   (*Day's Work.*) — A fanciful
tale, reminding one of Du Maurier's *Peter Ibbetson.*
From early childhood George Cottar had mysterious dreams
which invariably connected themselves with certain downs
bordering on a strange sea.   His rides and voyages had
always the same starting-place — a brushwood pile near the
beach.   And his constant companion was a girl who retained the same personality, though she grew in years.
George developed from a visionary boy into an athletic col-

legian and a gallant army officer, but in his dreams he was ever the Brushwood Boy. He returned to England and met society. Finally he saw a girl strikingly like his sleep-companion. It proved to be she, and her dreams were found to have matched his own in all respects. As they had loved one another in fancy they came to do so in reality.

"Exquisite in poetic spirituality." — *McClure's* (*editorial*).

"'The Brushwood Boy' is not a particularly good story, but it is the clearest sketch we have seen of Mr. Kipling's ideal young man, — his Galahad up to date, — who keeps himself clean in mind and body, and loves only when his appointed time comes, once and for all." — *Spectator.*

BUBBLING WELL ROAD. (*Life's Handicap.*) — The author loses his way in a patch of "plumed jungle grass, . . . from ten to twenty feet high, and from three to four miles square." In the heart of the patch, whither he has gone with the purpose of boar hunting, he comes upon the bubbling well, whence strange laughter and a devilish echo emanate, and where mysterious shapes appear. The natives believe the vicinity to be full of devils and ghosts. The adventurer's escape to open country is effected through the aid of a one-eyed priest, not the least remarkable of his discoveries.

BY THE HOOF OF THE WILD GOAT UP-TOSSED. — The first line of the lyric preceding "To be Filed for Reference" (*q.v.*), and purporting to be taken "from the unpublished papers of McIntosh Jellaludin."

BY WORD OF MOUTH. (*Plain Tales.*) — Not long after Dumoise, a civil surgeon, had lost his wife by typhoid, his bearer in great excitement reported that he had seen the *Memsahib*, who had said, "Give my *salaams* to the *Sahib*, and tell him that I shall meet him next month at Nuddea." Nuddea was over twelve hundred miles south of his station. Was it a coincidence that the doctor was unexpectedly transferred to Nuddea on special duty? There was an outbreak of cholera there. Soon after his arrival he succumbed to it, and thus joined the *Memsahib*.

"CAPTAINS COURAGEOUS" : A STORY OF THE GRAND BANKS. [New York and London, 1897. Before publication in book form by the *Century Company* it had appeared serially in *McClure's Magazine*. The title of the story is evidently quoted from the old English ballad of "Mary Ambree," Reliques of Ancient English Poetry, Vol. II. ("When captaines couragious," etc., p. 230.)] Harvey Cheyne, spoiled child of an American millionaire, overbalances himself while leaning in a fit of seasickness over the deck railing of an American liner, and is swept into the ocean. He is picked up by a dory from a Gloucester fishing-schooner, "We're Here," commanded by Disko Troop, a man of much shrewdness and rude strength of character. The latter declines to believe Harvey's tales of his father's wealth, and instead of landing this "most unlicked cub in fiction" at New York, as the boy desires, keeps him on the schooner until the close of the fishing-season, paying him ten dollars a month for working with the other deck hands. The rough discipline, sometimes enforced with the rope-end, which Harvey receives, proves to be his moral and physical salvation. When the season's end restores him to his parents, who have been heart-broken over his supposed death, he is a sturdy, self-respecting young fellow who has learned the lessons of industry and obedience. His father rewards Troop by giving his son, Dan, a chance to rise as a sailor. *" Captains Courageous "* is a boy's book ; that is to say (in the words of the *Edinburgh Review*), "it is a fine and healthy book for boys of all ages from eight to eighty." Novel in the strict sense it is not, nor does it aim to be. It has, however, been justly called "the most vivid and picturesque treatment of New England fishermen that has yet been made." (*Atlantic Monthly*, December, 1897.) Its plot is slight ; its incidents are neither numerous nor exciting ; its characterization for the most part is sketchy. Description is the book's strong point. Whether Mr. Kipling knows all regions of the seven seas equally well may be doubted, but he unquestionably knows the Grand Banks. The very breath and swing of the ocean is in the tale, and a bewildering amount of nautical lore of all sorts. Moreover, the book, while wholly without didacticism, is profoundly moral. It preaches in every line the author's favorite Gospel of Work.

"A series of literary sea-pieces constitute the value of the book from an artistic point of view." —*Athenæum*.

"One of the best things its author has done." — *Edinburgh Review*.

"The worst a hostile critic could say of ' *Captains Courageous*' would be to call it a glorified boy's book." — *London Times*.

"Never before has Mr. Kipling made more living characters, and never before has he described so well the vast waste spaces of the sea. . . . The book is, in truth, a sea-book, and from first to last the lap of the

waves against a boat's side and the humming of waters
are in our ears. '*Captains Courageous*' is as much
the book of the sea as Venice is her city. . . . Its moral
is beyond praise, for it teaches the great lesson that
obedience and the power to take orders and execute
them loyally and without any false sense of pride is essential to a well-ordered and happy life. . . .
Throughout the book Mr. Kipling's style and treatment
of his subject are masterly. . . . Not a word in the
book is out of tone." — *Spectator.*

" A great story, great in its massive simplicity, great
in its vital interest, its wealth of humor, its lessons of
humanity and democracy, its pathos and its nobility."
— *Nathan Haskell Dole in Book Buyer.*

"Like *Robinson Crusoe*, *Treasure Island*, and
one or two other first-rate books of adventure, it will
give almost as much pleasure to grown-up people as to
boys. . . . The interest of the book does not depend
by any means entirely on the story, but almost equally
on the vivid descriptions of the cod-fishing fleet and its
industry." — *Literature.*

Adverse judgments are expressed by the editor of the
(American) *Bookman*, who finds the book " meaning-
less" (" Mr. Kipling at the Crossroads," *Bookman*,
December, 1898), and by an anonymous reviewer in the
Atlantic, who says of the story, after praising its health
of atmosphere and serenity of manner, " ' *Captains
Courageous*' is badly wrought and is less than the
measure of his (Kipling's) power." (" Notable Recent
Novels," *Atlantic, December*, 1897.)

CELLS.   (*Ballads.*) — The song of a Tommy who is
confined to " the Clink " for " a thundering drink, and
blacking the corporal's eye." He has one consolation :

" I left my mark on the corporal's face, and I think he'll keep it there ! "

CHILDREN OF THE ZODIAC. (*Many Inventions.*) — The children of the Zodiac are the Ram, the Bull, the Lion, the Twins, and the Girl (Virgo). The principal actors are Leo and the Girl, who, after leading the life of gods, come to share earth conditions, and learn the mystery of love and the meaning of death. Though the setting of the story is fanciful, the *motif* is Kipling's favorite one : Each must do the day's work assigned him with brave patience. Or, in the concluding words of the allegory, " What comes or does not come, we must not be afraid."

> " In ' Children of the Zodiac ' there is a defence and justification of preaching such as St. Paul himself might say amen to." — *W. B. Parker, Public Opinion.*
>
> For adverse estimates of the story see *Academy*, July 1, 1893 ; also *Athenæum*, July 8, 1893. The latter review finds it obscure and wearisome, and thinks it the " one failure in the whole collection."

CHIL'S SONG. (*Second Jungle Book.*) — A poem following " Red Dog " in the *Second Jungle Book*. It is the song which Chil sang " as the kites dropped down one after another to the river-bed," when the great fight with the pack of dholes was finished.

CHOLERA CAMP. (*The Seven Seas.*) — A song full of rude pathos. There is cholera in the camp, with a death-roll of ten a day.

CITY OF DREADFUL NIGHT, THE. (*Life's Handicap.*) — A description of a fierce night in August at Lahore. Crowded roof-tops, Muezzin's midnight call, unburied corpses, snoring kites, lean dogs, sleeping lepers, scudding jackals, — all are photographed unforgettably.

"As a description it is wonderfully vivid and convincing." — *Spectator.*

"A truly wonderful piece of word-painting." — *Athenæum.*

"Never was there a more astonishing picture." — *Blackwoods.*

(See *From Sea to Sea.*)

CLEARED. (*Ballads.*) — An invective against certain men high in official life who instigated a notorious shooting affair in Ireland, which had wide-reaching political effects. The whitewashing Commission "cleared" these "honorable gentlemen" from the stigma of complicity in the crime, but an honest Englishman holds them to be worse even than the assassins.

"As a piece of deadly, logical, impassioned invective, 'Cleared' may scarce be matched." — *National Observer.*

"Rings false from first line to last." — *Francis Adams in Fortnightly.*

COME BACK TO ME, BELOVED, OR I DIE! — The refrain of Bisesa's song, which begins,

"Alone upon the housetops, to the North
I turn and watch the lightning in the sky."

(See "Beyond the Pale," *Plain Tales from the Hills.*)

CONFERENCE OF THE POWERS, A. (*Many Inventions.*) — Mr. Eustace Cleever, novelist, falls into the company of three young fellows home from the army. This self-complacent "decorator and colorman in words" has never been ten miles from fellow-Englishmen, and has been wont to regard warfare as unnatural if not essentially vulgar. Always ready to draw out men in search of "material," he encourages the youths to talk of raids and battles. He ends by learning a good many things, and confesses that he has "been moving in worlds not realized."

CONSEQUENCES. (*Plain Tales.*) — Celebrates Mrs. Hauksbee's cleverness, and the audacity of one Tarrion, who, with that lady's help, obtained possession of secret information useful to the Government, and, armed therewith, demanded and received a fat appointment.

CONUNDRUM OF THE WORKSHOPS, THE. (*Ballads.*) — A poem expressing scorn for merely professional critics, — the slaves of form and tradition, — who insist on asking about work which they admit to be clever, striking, or human, "Yes, but is it *art* ?"

"A charming satire." — *Academy*.

CONVERSION OF AURELIAN McGOGGIN, THE. (*Plain Tales.*) — McGoggin was "all head, no physique, and a hundred theories," which latter he exploited on all occasions. He worked nine hours a day in the Indian summer, and finally collapsed. The break-down took the form of *aphasia*, which caused loss of speech and memory. After three months of rest he recovered, but he was cured of his intellectual conceit. Something had at last happened which he couldn't understand.

COURTING OF DINAH SHADD, THE. (*Life's Handicap.*) — Mulvaney tells of his first meeting with Dinah Shadd, and of the progress, not always smooth-running, of the courtship. After his engagement Judy Sheehy inveigles him into drunken protestations of affection, and afterwards tries to prove that he is her "promised man." In this plot she is ably backed up by Mother Sheehy, a broadly comic character, who, when she finds that Mulvaney remains true to Dinah, curses both him and his sweetheart with Irish volubility.   But Dinah Shadd remains constant.

"A little masterpiece." — *Francis Adams in Fort-nightly.*

"The one story in the book [L. H.] admirable from first to last is 'The Courting of Dinah Shadd.'" — *Lionel Johnson in Academy.*

CUPID'S ARROWS. (*Plain Tales.*) — A beautiful girl without fortune was shown attention by a very ugly but rich commissioner in Simla.   Mamma was overjoyed, but daughter, while flattered, vastly preferred young Cubbon, a handsome dragoon with no prospects.   The commissioner arranged an archery tournament for ladies, with a diamond-studded bracelet as prize.   All could see that the bracelet was a gift to the girl, who was the champion archer there-abouts, and that acceptance carried with it the heart and hand of the great man.   The contest came.   The girl deliberately shot wild and lost the prize, mamma wept with shame and disappointment, and the boy carried the real prize away after all.

"The archery contest in 'Cupid's Arrows' needs only to be compared with a similar scene in *Daniel Deronda* to show how much more closely Mr. Kipling keeps his eye on details than George Eliot did." — *Edmund Gosse.*

DANNY DEEVER. (*Ballads.*) — A powerfully realistic ballad.   Danny Deever was hanged in the presence of his regiment for having shot a sleeping comrade.

Edmund C. Stedman speaks of "the originality and weird power" of this poem, and Lionel Johnson pronounces it in the *Academy* "the most poetical, in the sense of being the most imaginative and heightened in expression," of the *Barrack-Room Ballads.*

DARZEE'S CHAUNT. — Verses following "Rikki-Tikki-Tavi" in the *Jungle Book*. The song is sung by Darzee, the tailor-bird, in honor of the mongoose, Rikki-Tikki-Tavi, who has killed the cobras.

DAUGHTER OF THE REGIMENT, THE. (*Plain Tales.*) — Miss Jhansi McKenna was plain, ill dressed, and Irish, but she was the daughter of the regiment and the pride of B Company. Mulvaney tells the story of the cholera scourge, and the heroic efforts made on behalf of the men by Ould Pummeloe, Jhansi's mother, and by Jhansi herself, then a little girl, who followed the old woman, carrying water to the boys. Ould Pummeloe died, but Jhansi remained in the regiment. Mulvaney was her self-appointed champion and protector, and it was he who brought about her marriage with a corporal.

DEDICATION TO THE CITY OF BOMBAY. (*The Seven Seas.*) — The opening poem in *The Seven Seas*, giving expression to the author's pride in his native city, —

"For I was born in her gate,
Between the palms and the sea,
Where the world-end steamers wait."

DEDICATORY POEM. (*Ballads.*) — These lines, addressed to Wolcott Balestier, touch almost the high-water mark of Kipling's work. They have no title, but will be recalled from their opening verse:

"Beyond the path of the outmost sun, through utter darkness hurled."

For a detailed analysis, see the *N. Y. Independent*, March 30, 1899. An adverse critical estimate of the poem may be found in Mr. Lionel Johnson's review of *Barrack-Room Ballads* in the London *Academy*.

DEPARTMENTAL DITTIES. — (Published, Lahore, 1886; second and third editions, Lahore; fourth edition, Calcutta; subsequent editions, Calcutta and London; pirated editions, New York and elsewhere. See Bibliography.) A volume of local satires, parodies, and society verse. Since Mr. Kipling has not included the book among his collected works, the poems are not in this primer given separate consideration under their titles.[1] As a matter of fact, they are hardly worth it. The best of them, in our judgment, are entitled, The Story of Uriah, The Galley Slave, and What the People Said. The full list of poems in the first Calcutta edition (1890) follows : *Departmental Ditties.* — Prelude ("I have eaten your bread and salt"); General Summary ; Army Headquarters ; Study of an Elevation, in Indian Ink ; A Legend of the Foreign Office ; The Story of Uriah ; The Post that Fitted ; Public Waste ; Delilah ; What Happened ; Pink Dominoes ; The Man who could Write ; Municipal ; A Code of Morals ; The Last Department. *Other Verses.* — To the Unknown Goddess ; The Rupaiyat of Omar Kal'vin ; La Nuit Blanche ; My Rival ; The Lovers' Litany ; A Ballad of Burial ; Divided Destinies ; The Masque of Plenty ; The Mare's Nest ; Possibilities ; Christmas in India ; Pagett, M.P. ; The Song of the Women ; A Ballade of Jakko Hill ; The Plea of the Simla Dancers ; The Ballad of Fisher's Boarding House ; As the Bell Clinks ; Certain Maxims of Hafiz ; The Grave of the Hundred Head ; The

---

[1] As the *Kipling Primer* goes to press we learn that an authorized edition of the *Ditties* is just issued by Mr. Kipling's New York publishers. This fact does not, however, alter our conviction that these juvenile verses hardly deserve separate consideration.

Moon of Other Days; The Overland Mail; What the People Said; The Undertaker's Horse; The Fall of Jock Gillespie; An Old Song; Arithmetic on the Frontier; One Viceroy Resigns; The Betrothed; A Tale of Two Cities; Griffin's Debt; In Spring Time; Two Months: (1) In June, (2) In September; The Galley Slave; L'Envoi.

DERELICT, THE. (*The Seven Seas.*) — The song of a ship, wrecked and abandoned at sea, mourning her lost estate.

DESTROYERS, THE. — A poem of nine double quatrains contributed to *McClure's* for May, 1898. This spirited description of torpedoes as used in modern warfare opens :

"The strength of twice three thousand horse
   That seek the single goal."

Possibly the most striking lines are :

"The brides of death that wait the groom —
   The choosers of the slain."

DEVIL AND THE DEEP SEA, THE. (*Day's Work.*) — A British whaling-steamer, the "Haliotis," won a bad reputation by piratical and poaching expeditions, and was finally captured in tropical waters, her holds filled with stolen pearls.   A foreign man-of-war signalled her to "heave to."   Its order being disobeyed, it fired a shot which disabled her engines.   The "Haliotis" was then towed to the nearest port, and the crew, forbidden access to their consul, were marched into the back country and there impressed into the army.   The British Government demanded apologies and reparation.   The men were grudgingly released and supplied with provisions, but were at last removed to the "Haliotis," which rode at anchor in the harbor, stripped of everything except its wrecked engines. Wardrop, the Scotch engineer, was equal to the exigency. How he patched up the machinery with the aid of his naked, half-starved associates, how the boat made her escape under her own steam, and how she met her final fate — these facts are related with great skill.

DISTURBER OF TRAFFIC, THE. (*Many Inventions.*) — A powerful study of the growth of madness in the brain of one Dowse, a lonely lighthouse keeper, stationed at Flores Strait in the Java seas. Hardly less remarkable is the rapidly-sketched portrait of Challong, the "sea-gypsy" Caliban with "webby-foot-hands," Dowse's sole companion. The story is concerned with the wild conduct into which Dowse was led by his insanity, with his rescue, and with his subsequent cure.

> "In ' The Disturber of Traffic ' Mr. Kipling gives us one of those inimitable sketches of blended farce and pathos that he alone seems able to contrive." — *Academy.*

DOVE OF DACCA, THE. (*Ballads.*) — An Indian Rajah, on setting forth to battle, left word that if a "dove of flight" he took with him should return, it might be taken as a sign that he was defeated, and thereupon his palace should be burned, lest his foemen take it as a spoil of war. He was victorious, but the homesick dove, escaping, flew home before he could overtake it. He found his orders carried out. His palace was in ashes.

DRAY WARA YOW DEE. (*In Black and White.*) — A native, having found his wife unfaithful, has killed her, and is devoting the rest of his life to the capture and punishment of the guilty lover. The man is a devout Mussulman, but regards the fulfilment of his vengeance as a religious duty. "When I have accomplished the matter and my honor is made clean I shall return thanks unto God, the Holder of the Scale of the Law, and I shall sleep."

DREAM OF DUNCAN PARRENNESS, THE. (*Life's Handicap.*) — A dissolute youth dreams that a man enters his chamber and replies, when ordered angrily to leave, that a youth of the other's kidney need fear neither man nor devil, and that as brave a fellow was like enough to become Governor-General. But for all this, he adds, the young man must pay the price. As he turns his eyes on Duncan, the lad is horrified to discover that this man of the evil face is himself grown older. The tormentor then demands in turn the youth's trust in man, faith in woman, and boy's soul and conscience. In return he leaves something in Duncan's hand. At dawn the boy looks at the gift. It is a morsel of dry bread.

DRUMS OF THE FORE AND AFT, THE. (*Wee Willie Winkie.*) — A story of the heroism of two fourteen-year-old boys. One was a London gutter-snipe, neither could give much account of his parentage, both fought each other and all comers, swore, smoked, and drank. But when their regiment, made up of raw recruits, were for the first time in action, and had broken and fled before the long-knifed Afghans, it was the two drummer-boys who marched side by side straight into the enemy's front, urging forward their cowardly comrades to the tune of the " British Grenadier." The boys dropped at the first volley, but the English rallied and carried the day.

" 'The Drums of the Fore and Aft ' is one of those performances which are apt to reduce criticism to the

mere tribute of a respectful admiration.   It is absolutely
and thoroughly well done." — *Francis Adams in
Fortnightly*.

" By far the most powerful and ingenious story which
Mr. Kipling has yet dedicated to a study of childhood."
— *Edmund Gosse, Century*, 1891.

" ' The Drums of the Fore and Aft ' is an epic which
has seized upon every man from the age of ten upwards."
Blackwoods.

'EATHEN, THE.   (*The Seven Seas.*) — A barrack-room
ballad.

EDUCATION OF OTIS YEERE, THE.   (*Under the Deodars.*) — This tale has for its motive the failure of a pla-
tonic friendship.   Mrs. Hauksbee attempts to act the rôle
of " guide, philosopher, and friend " toward Otis Yeere,
a thoroughly honest but commonplace and discouraged
man.   Her purpose is only half selfish.   She desires to
draw the man out of himself, to inspire in him new confidence in his abilities and new interest in life.   He repays
her by falling madly in love.   When she repulses his
advances angrily, he is completely crushed.

" Mrs. Hauksbee and Mrs. Mallowe are neither edi-
fying nor — shall we venture to breathe the heresy ? —
amusing companions.   Their cynicism palls upon us, and
their occasional lapses into womanliness fail to be convincing.   ' The Education of Otis Yeere ' and ' A
Second Rate Woman ' . . . are clever and caustic
enough, no doubt, but they leave a disagreeable taste in
the mouth." — *Athenæum*.

ENGLISH FLAG, THE.   (*Ballads.*) — In reply to the
question, " What is the Flag of England ?   Winds of the
World, declare ! " — the North, South, East, and West

Winds make answer in turn. The result is one of the most spirited poems Kipling has given us. Mr. Lionel Johnson, in the *Academy*, finds it "grievously spoiled," however, "by exaggeration of tone."

ENLIGHTENMENTS OF PAGETT, M.P. (Added in the *Outward Bound* edition, to *In Black and White*.) Mr. Pagett, Member of Parliament, is possessed of much self-complacency and of many decided theories about India. Both are considerably shaken after a visit to his old school-friend Orde, now an English official in Amara. Pagett's especial hobby is the desirability of bestowing electoral institutions on the people, but he is shown first that they do not desire these, and second that they could not or would not exercise such privileges if they had them. The reforms needed are far more fundamental. This sketch aims to expose the fallacy of Liberal positions ; so too does "The Head of the District" (*q.v.*).

EVARRA AND HIS GODS. (*Ballads.*) — An allegorical poem in blank verse relating to the experiences on earth and in Paradise of Evarra, "Maker of Gods in lands beyond the seas."

EXPLANATION, THE. (*Ballads.*) — Once on a time the arrows in the quivers of Love and of Death became so mixed that neither could distinguish his own darts from those of his enemy. "Thus it was they wrought our woe."

FALSE DAWN. (*Plain Tales.*) — Two sisters who resemble each other very closely are in love with the same man. He himself prefers the younger one and means to propose to her at a moonlight riding-picnic. A furious dust-storm arises and adds to the darkness. The man, mistaking her for her sister, proposes to the elder girl and is accepted.   When he discovers his mistake he is distracted with fear and shame, but explanations, awkward and humiliating, follow at sunrise, and the party ride homeward.

FEET OF THE YOUNG MEN, THE. — A poem of eight stanzas with chorus, contributed by Kipling to the Christmas (1897) number of *Scribner's Magazine*.   It is dedicated "to the memory of the late W. Hallett-Phillips."

FINANCES OF THE GODS, THE. (*Life's Handicap.*) — A tale of the gods told by a Hindu to a child.   It relates how a miserly money-lender, in trying to outwit Shiv and Ganesh and to rob a poor mendicant under their protection, was caught in his own snares.

FINEST STORY IN THE WORLD, THE. (*Many Inventions.*) — A romance of reincarnation.   Kipling makes the acquaintance of a youth who thinks himself poet and tale-writer, but who is really without talent.   One thing, however, marks Charlie Mears from other bank-clerks with aspirations.   He has been a Greek galley slave in some former life and tosses about bits of priceless experience with the impression that they are nothing more than inventions of his fancy.   The novelist knows better, and beguiles Charlie into talking, under the hope that he can secure matter for an immortal romance.   Things are going well, when the chain of recollections is finally snapped, and the boy is lost.   Charlie has "tasted the love of woman that kills remembrance ; " the finest story in the world will never be written.

> "The scheme is ambitious in the highest degree, and its execution extraordinarily successful." — *Saturday Review.*

" It is a pity that so masterly a writer should give his name to such unfinished work as ' The Finest Story in the World.' " — *Spectator*.

" Ingenious and interesting, but not wholly satisfactory." — *Athenæum*.

" A romance for sheer photographic realization bad to beat." — *Gentleman's Magazine*.

" The psychological skill of ' The Finest Story in the World ' is . . . remarkable." — *Academy*.

FIRST CHANTEY, THE.   (*The Seven Seas.*) — A ballad of primitive man.   A pair of lovers, fleeing from the wrath of the woman's tribe, were miraculously delivered from their pursuers by the aid of the Wind God and the Sun.

" ' The First Chantey ' needs a second reading, and repays it." — *Academy*.

FLEET IN BEING, A. — A series of descriptive articles published in the *Morning Post* (London) in the latter part of 1898, and subsequently issued in book form, which were the outcome of Mr. Kipling's cruise with the Channel squadron in the fall of the same year.   Perhaps a sufficient comment on these brilliant letters may be found in the following communication from Mr. Clarke Russell :

" *To the Editor of the Morning Post* (*London*) :

" SIR: I have been reading Mr. Kipling's contributions entitled *A Fleet in Being* with the greatest enjoyment and profit.

" A naval officer said to me:

" ' If Rudyard Kipling had been born in a battle-ship, if all his life he had drilled with the marines, stoked with the stokers, and hauled with the Jackies at the falls, loaded and fired every gun aboard ship, conned the vessel on the bridge, grasped the spokes of the wheel, chaffed and argued in the gun-room, and in

the ward-room listened with respectful countenance, he
could not have known more about it.'

"W. CLARK RUSSELL.

"9 SYDNEY PLACE, BATH, Nov. 11, 1898."

FLOWERS, THE. (*The Seven Seas.*) — A song in praise
and defence of the flora of Colonial Britain, however exotic
these alien posies may appear to the cockney and stay-at-
home. The lyric was called out by the following very
unsympathetic comment in *The Athenæum*: "To our
private taste there is always something a little exotic,
almost artificial, in songs which, under an English aspect
and dress, are yet so manifestly the product of other skies.
They affect us like translations; the very fauna and flora are
alien, remote ; the dog's-tooth violet is but an ill substitute
for the rathe primrose, nor can we ever believe that the
wood-robin sings as sweetly in April as the English thrush."

FOLLOW ME 'OME. (*The Seven Seas.*) — A soldier's
honest lament for a dead comrade :

" 'E was all that I 'ad in the way of a friend."

FOR TO ADMIRE. (*The Seven Seas.*) — A barrack-
room ballad.

FORD O' KABUL RIVER. (*Ballads.*) — A British soldier
mourns the death of a comrade drowned at the Ford of
Kabul river.

FOURTH DIMENSION, THE. (*Day's Work.*) — A rich
young American residing in England desires to reach London in great haste, and orders his butler to signal the first
down train. On attempting to board the express, however, he meets with forcible resistance, is dragged, after a
struggle, into the guard's van, and at the terminus of the
line is jailed. He is fined and set free, but the flagging of

a train is a more serious offence than assault, and the Railway pursues him with a voluminous correspondence and the setting in motion of legal machinery. He receives visits from lawyers who talk about precedents, and from doctors who investigate his sanity. He is released only after much expense of good temper and red tape, and of explanations on the part of an English friend. On returning to New York he has lost every trace of the Anglomania which once characterized him.

FRIEND'S FRIEND, A. (*Plain Tales.*) — A friend, against whom the author vows vengeance, sent a letter introducing an acquaintance of his and saying that any kindness shown the visitor would be counted a personal favor. The acquaintance was entertained at the Club and taken to the Afghan Ball. Here he became hilariously drunk and disgraced his host before all the guests. After the ball the drunken man was dressed in a very original costume and bundled into a bullock-cart which carried him away. He never came back.

FROM SEA TO SEA. — A collection in two volumes of the special correspondence and occasional articles, mainly letters of travel, contributed by Mr. Kipling to the Lahore *Civil and Military Gazette* and the Allahabad *Pioneer* between 1887 and 1889. It includes, in their order, (1) *Letters of Marque,* nineteen sketches descriptive of a journey through Rajputana, November–December, 1887 ; (2) *From Sea to Sea,* thirty-seven letters, mainly descriptive of Japan and the United States, and including the sketches published in the latter country in an incorrect and fragmentary form and without authorization, under the title *American Notes,* March–September, 1889 ; (3) *The City of*

Dreadful Night (not to be confounded with the sketch included in *Life's Handicap*), a series of eight articles depicting the darker side of Calcutta, whose worst haunts were penetrated by Mr. Kipling, accompanied by the city police ; (4) *Among the Railway Folk*, three letters descriptive of Jemalpur, the headquarters of the East India Railway ; (5) *The Giridih Coal-Fields*, three letters ; (6) *In an Opium Factory*, an article occupying seven pages and concerned with the manufacture of opium in the Ghazipur factory, on the banks of the Ganges ; and (7) *The Smith Administration*, a collection of eighteen stories and sketches contributed by Mr. Kipling to his newspaper between 1887 and 1888. Their titles follow : The Cow-house Jirga ; A Bazaar Dhulip ; The Hands of Justice ; The Serai Cabal ; The Story of a King ; The Great Census ; The Killing of Hatim Tai ; A Self-made Man ; The Vengeance of Lal Beg ; Hunting a Miracle ; The Explanation of Mir Baksh ; A Letter from Golam Singh ; The Writing of Yakub Khan ; A King's Ashes ; The Bride's Progress ; A District at Play, What it Comes To ; The Opinions of Gunner Barnabas.

The initial stories of *The Smith Administration* are written in the first person by one Smith, who, in governing a household of native servants, fancifully calls himself a king, and, adopting all the cant of royal parlance, speaks of himself as the Supreme Government, the State, and the like. This device is somewhat awkwardly carried out, and when it is wholly dropped, as in some of the stories, the gain in effectiveness is notable.

It would be ungracious to find fault with the juvenile tone of many of the letters in *From Sea to Sea*. Such of them as had been put between covers in Mr. Kipling's early period were long ago suppressed by their author. He was forced to their republication, as he says, " by the enterprise of various publishers who, not content with disinterring old newspaper work from the decent seclusion of the office files, have in several instances seen fit to embellish it with additions and interpolations."

FUZZY–WUZZY. (*Ballads.*) — Tommy Atkins's tribute to the fighting qualities of Fuzzy-Wuzzy, the savage Soudanese warrior, —

   " 'E rushes at the smoke when we let drive,
     An', before we know, 'e's 'ackin' at our 'ead ;
   'E's all 'ot sand an' ginger when alive,
     An' 'e's generally shammin' when 'e's dead."

    " No single ballad has had such a *furore* of success as ' Fuzzy-Wuzzy.' " — *Francis Adams, Fortnightly,* 1893.

GATE OF THE HUNDRED SORROWS, THE. (*Plain Tales.*) — The confession of an opium slave six weeks before he died. The man describes with convincing realism the history of his five years' bondage, and gives us a picture of the opium den, " The Gate of the Hundred Sorrows," which has come to be his only home.

    " From ' The Gate of the Hundred Sorrows ' more is to be gleaned of the real action of opium-smoking, and the causes of that indulgence, than from many sapient debates in the British House of Commons." — *Edmund Gosse.*

    " Defeats DeQuincey on his own ground." — *Andrew Lang.*

GEMINI. (*In Black and White.*) — The twins are Durga Dass and Ram Dass, whom no one can tell apart.

Durga Dass complains to an English Sahib that he has
been badly used by his brother. Ram Dass has incurred
the resentment of a wealthy landholder who incites his
servants to waylay and beat him. The servants mistake
Durga for his brother, and abuse him cruelly. He falls
violently ill. Ram Dass professes sympathy and promises
aid in gaining justice from the Courts. Instead of doing
so, he secures false witnesses, pretends to the authorities
that he himself has been attacked, and wins a judgment of
five hundred rupees. Not content with this, he robs his
brother of his savings and absconds with the booty.

" ' Gemini ' is a most laughable version of the *Comedy
of Errors*." — *Quarterly.*

GENTLEMEN–RANKERS. (*Ballads.*) — The reflections,
proud, bitter, and despairing, of an Englishman, bred and
educated as a gentleman, but now a drunken trooper of the
Empress, " damned from here to Eternity."

The *Saturday Review* thought this the only " positive failure in the volume."

GEORGIE PORGIE. (*Life's Handicap.*) — " Georgie
Porgie " held an appointment in Upper Burmah, and being
lonely took unto himself a native wife. After three months
of domestic comfort he decided to wed some girl at home
who would not smoke cheroots and who could play a
piano. He obtained a six-months' leave, and sent
" Georgina " weeping to her father's house with promises
of his speedy return. From England Georgie brought back
an English wife and then went to a new station, whither
the Burmese girl, after tracking " her God " half over
India, at last followed him. On learning of his marriage,
her love was too unselfish to permit her to make herself
known. She went away broken-hearted.

GERM–DESTROYER, A. (*Plain Tales.*) — A Viceroy had an officious Secretary, whom he got rid of in this way. There were two men, Mellish, a cranky inventor of a powder to destroy cholera, and Mellishe, a rich grandee, stopping at the same hotel and both desirous of seeing the Viceroy. The Secretary in sending a dinner invitation to Mellishe left off the final *e* in his name. The Germ-destroyer accordingly accepted the invitation and nearly smoked out the Viceroy with the lighted powder. His Excellency told the joke on Wonder, the Secretary, on all occasions. "And I really tho't for a moment," he wound up, "that my dear good Wonder had hired an assassin to clear his way to the throne." Wonder saw the point ; he found his health suddenly giving way, and resigned his post.

GIFT OF THE SEA, THE. (*Ballads.*) — A fisherman's widow sits by the shroud of her dead baby. From outside the cottage drifts the sound of an infant's wailing. Believing it to be her own child's soul crying out as it " waits to pass," she delays investigating the origin of the voice. Finally she discovers a newly-dead child on the shore, who might have taken the place of her own had she rescued it in time.

GIPSY TRAIL, THE. — A lyric of thirteen four-line stanzas which appeared in the *Century* for December, 1892.

GIRIDIH COAL–FIELDS, THE. (See *From Sea to Sea.*)

GOD FROM THE MACHINE, THE. (*Soldiers Three.*) — In the days when Mulvaney was a " Corp'ril," the Colonel's daughter was in love with Captain Broom, "a tricky man an' a liar by natur'," who had won her consent to an elopement. Mulvaney, engaged in shifting scenes for an amateur play in which the two were actors, overheard, by persistent eavesdropping, the full plot. His method of preventing its accomplishment forms the basis of a very amusing tale, told in his own words.

GUNGA DIN.   (*Ballads.*) — A tribute to the regimental water-carrier —

> " The uniform 'e wore
> Was nothin' much before,
> An' rather less than 'arf o' that be'ind."

And yet, among other good characteristics :

> " 'E didn't seem to know the use o' fear."

Gunga's unselfish performance of duty, and manly death on the battlefield, raise the poor fellow into the heroic type.   One of Kipling's masterpieces.

> " ' Gunga Din ' is one of the very finest of the *Ballads.*" — *Francis Adams in Fortnightly.*
>
> " Much as we delight in ' Fuzzy-Wuzzy,' our especial favorite in all Mr. Kipling's work is ' Gunga Din.'   It has the unequalled lilt of Kipling at his best." — *Athenæum.*

HAUNTED SUBALTERNS.   (Added to *Plain Tales from the Hills* in the *Outward Bound* edition.) — Horrocks and Tesser, subalterns in the " Inextinguishables," were either haunted by ghosts or possessed by devils.   Otherwise somebody must have carried out so successful a practical joke that the mystery of the White Things and the Banjo that played itself could never be unravelled, which is hardly possible.

HEAD OF THE DISTRICT, THE.   (*Life's Handicap.*) — Yardley-Orde, deputy commissioner of a wild border district, died of fever. The Khusru Kheyl were insubordinate ; it was only the strong hand of the deputy that had held the tribe in check. The blunder was made of appointing as the Englishman's successor a native Bengali, Grish Chunder Dé. This story is a record of the fatal consequences.

> " ' The Head of the District ' sums up, in its two dozen pages, the whole question of Indian administration." — *Athenæum.*

HER MAJESTY'S SERVANTS. (*Jungle Book.*) — Observations on army and camp life from the point of view of a baggage-camel, a troop-horse, Billy, the mule, Two Tails, the elephant, and a pair of gun-bullocks, who conduct a conversation in the writer's hearing.

HILL OF ILLUSION, THE. (*Under the Deodars.*) — What promises to be a Launcelot and Guinevere affair is prevented by Guinevere's withdrawal from the contract just before the projected flight. "It can't last," she explains ; "you'll get angry, and then you'll swear, and then you'll get jealous, and then you'll mistrust me, — you do now !" This dramatic sketch in dialogue has almost no plot, but it develops a very subtle psychological situation.

> "A masterpiece of analysis and penetration." — *Blackwoods.*

> "Contains the most admirably sustained piece of dialogue he (Kipling) has yet written." — *Francis Adams, Fortnightly, November,* 1891.

HIS CHANCE IN LIFE. (*Plain Tales.*) — Michele D'Cruze was a telegraph signaller with small wages but much pride — for one-eighth of his blood was white. He desired to wed a nurse-girl, also of mixed blood, whose mother consented to the marriage only on condition that

Michele should earn at least fifty rupees a month. Shortly afterward he was transferred to Tibasu, a little sub-office, and there his chance came. The Hindus and Mahommedans started a riot, which Michele, acting as the only representative of English authority in the place, promptly put down. As a reward, he was transferred to a sixty-six-rupee post, and his marriage soon followed.

His Majesty the King. (*Wee Willie Winkie.*) — His Majesty the King is a little boy whose father and mother have become estranged through a foolish misunderstanding. They have turned him over to a governess and are too busy with their separate occupations to pet the child. How the lonely boy longs for and finds companionship, how he unconsciously prevents his mother from entering into a ruinous intrigue, and later is the cause of uniting, over his sick-bed, the hearts of his parents in new love for each other and for him, — these are some of the things the story-writer describes for us.

His Private Honour. (*Many Inventions.*) — A young lieutenant strikes Ortheris on parade. The latter, though furiously angry, screens the offender by lying about the matter to the commanding officer ; but he broods savagely on his wrong. Ortheris finally gains ''satisfaction,'' and ends by pronouncing his enemy '' a gentleman all over.'' The narrative of the fight between Ouless and Ortheris in the high grass of the jungle is given with great humor and spirit.

'' A brisker tale was never penned.'' — *Athenæum.*

His Wedded Wife. (*Plain Tales.*) — A Senior Sub-altern badgered the life out of a pretty, boyish comrade, fresh from Home, until the latter laid a wager that he would work a sell on his tormentor which the man wouldn't forget.   One night, dressed as a lady, the younger man, in the presence of all the Mess, came upon the Senior Subaltern, who had recently announced his marriage engagement, and, sobbing, threw his arms about the other's neck, greeting him as "my darling" and "husband." So perfectly was the part of the neglected wife acted that all failed to penetrate the disguise.   The thing had assumed almost a serious air when the actor announced his identity and demanded the money he had won.

How Fear Came. (*Second Jungle Book.*) — In the early days of the Jungle, Fear was unknown.   The beasts lived together unsuspiciously, nor as yet had any died. Their food was grass, leaves, and fruit.   But the First of the Tigers in a fit of fury killed a buck, thus bringing Death into the Jungle.   As a result the Jungle People were told that they should know Fear.   It was found in the form of Man, a hairless creature sitting in a cave.   His voice filled the beasts with terror, and they became even afraid one of the other.   But the Tiger determined to follow and slay the new enemy, thinking thus to destroy Fear forever.   On the Man's death, other creatures of his kind waged warfare against the Jungle People, and Fear was thenceforward never absent from them.

"The wild sweep of the narrative is inimitable." — *Joel Chandler Harris.*

Hunting–Song of the Seeonee Pack. — A three-stanza lyric following "Mowgli's Brothers" in the *Jungle Book*.   Its refrain is "Once, twice, and again!"

Hymn before Action. (*The Seven Seas.*) — An eloquent and devout appeal for aid to the "God of Battles."

" His is a healthy, austere, old-fashioned faith — the
faith of England and the Old Testament. The two
great utterances that we have had of it, ' The Recessional,' and the ' Hymn before Action,' are composed
of the words of the Psalmist and Milton and Cromwell.
They are both such hymns as David and Joshua might
have used." — *W. B. Parker in New World.*

IMPERIAL RESCRIPT, AN.   (*Ballads.*) — A short para-
ble giving us Kipling's view of present industrial conditions.
It is characterized by British horse sense, and faith in " the
God of Things as They Are."

IN AMBUSH. — A tale of school-boy escapades published
in *McClure's* for August, 1898. Stalky, McTurk, and
Beetle, introduced to the readers of *McClure's* in the
" Slaves of the Lamp " (August, 1897), and to reappear
in *Stalky and Co.*, are the principal actors.

IN AN OPIUM FACTORY.   (See *From Sea to Sea.*)

IN ERROR.   (*Plain Tales.*) — Moriarty, a civil engineer who has become secretly enslaved to the drink habit,
meets Mrs. Reiver, a thoroughly bad woman (*see* " The
Rescue of Pluffles "), and completely idealizes her. As a
tribute to the influence of this woman whom he regards
angelic, he masters his appetite. The question is, What
credit does Mrs. Reiver deserve for his reformation?

IN FLOOD TIME.   (*In Black and White.*) — The
warden of Barhwi Ford relates a story of his past life to a
Sahib who wishes to cross the stream. When a young
man he loved a Hindu girl who lived at Pateera, far down
the river, and thither every night the youth went to meet
his sweetheart among the crops. Another suitor won the
man's hatred, and he swam thereafter with a knife in his
belt. When the great Flood came, the lover kept his tryst

despite the wrath of the torrent. The most thrilling epi-
sode is that of the man's meeting with the corpse of his
rival in mid-stream and making use of it as a life-buoy.
This tale is one of Kipling's greatest triumphs.

    "This little story is quite a poem in prose ; it could
not be praised too highly." — *Edinburgh Review.*
    "The idyl of a dusky Hero and Leander. . . .
Enthralling." —*Athenæum.*

IN THE HOUSE OF SUDDHOO. (*Plain Tales.*) — Old
Suddhoo, whose son at Peshawar is very ill, falls into the
toils of a pretended sorcerer. The latter, getting a friend
to telegraph daily reports of the boy's condition, gives Suddhoo the impression, with the aid of uncanny conjuring
tricks, that the information is obtained by magic. After
the boy recovers, the father is still entirely under the influence of the magician, whom he continues to give large sums
of money, much to the disgust and anger of Janoo, the
daughter.

IN THE MATTER OF A PRIVATE. (*Soldiers Three.*) —
Crimes committed by British soldiers are often due to nothing more than hysteria. Private Simmons was made the
butt of his companions and was tormented especially by
one Losson, who added to his other insults that of a parrot
which he taught to call Simmons names. Simmons'
strained endurance finally snapped ; seizing his rifle he
shot Losson dead, and rushing away defied his pursuers. In
his madness he wounded a major and shot at a corporal.
Simmons was hanged. Press and public were shocked at
the criminality of the army. The Colonel attributed
Simmons' act to drink, and the chaplain to the devil.

    "The wonderful study of heat-hysteria, entitled, ' In
the Matter of a Private.' " — *Athenæum.*

IN THE NEOLITHIC AGE. (*Ballads.*) — A striking
satirical poem which enforces the truth that quarrelling over
different ways and means to produce an effect is foolish,
provided only the effect is produced :

"There are nine and sixty ways of constructing tribal
lays,
And every single one of them is right ! "

IN THE PRIDE OF HIS YOUTH. (*Plain Tales.*) — The
career of Dicky Hatt in India was handicapped by an
early and imprudent marriage. He was forced to practice
great economy in order to send home the desired allow-
ances. After his baby died his fretful wife wrote that if
certain things costing money had been done the child
might have been saved. The final blow was the news of
the woman's elopement with another man. Although
Dicky's hard work had meanwhile told, the offer of a
superior post was bitterly declined. His spirit was broken.

IN THE RUKH. (*Many Inventions.*) — Mowgli of the
Jungle Books reappears — now a grown man, a sort of
Eastern Donatello. Muller, the fat Dutchman, and Gisborne, sturdy forest officer, form a background for the
lightly-sketched child of nature, walking like a shadow,
wreathed with white flowers, taming wolf and wild pig.
His attachment to Sahib Gisborne, his detection of Abdul's
theft, his flight with the latter's daughter, and their subsequent marriage, — a wild birds' mating, — are deftly woven
into this charming narrative.

"The whole study is one of great subtilty, and
marked by a powerful restraint not usual in Mr.
Kipling's work. It closes with a love idyll of exquisite
beauty." — *Academy.*

Index to Writings   129

INCARNATION OF KRISHNA MULVANEY, THE. (*Life's Handicap.*) — Mulvaney becomes possessed of a gorgeous palanquin and marvellous adventures grow out of that ownership. Obtaining three days' leave "to see a friend," the Irishman hires bearers and departs in his royal chair, hoping to find a purchaser. An enemy pays off an old score by making Mulvaney drunk and putting him on a train bound for Benares, hoping thus to make him over-stay his leave and obtain martial discipline. But at Benares he has the luck to stumble upon a "Queens' Praying," and his palanquin being mistaken for that of a native queen he is carried to the temple of Prithi-Devi. Here his ready wit saves his life. Wrapping himself in the lining of the palanquin, he emerges from his prison, and in the half-light of the temple successfully impersonates the God Krishna. After imposing on the superstitious women and intimidating the priest, he escapes and returns to the regiment.

"What is 'The Incarnation of Krishna Mulvaney' but rollicking, incomparable, irresistible farce?" — *Blackwoods.*

JACKET, THE. (*The Seven Seas.*) — A barrack-room ballad.

"Represents the worst type of Mr. Kipling's ballads." — *Spectator.*

JEWS IN SHUSHAN. (*Life's Handicap.*) — A story of eight Hebrews in Shushan, a city in the north of India. When their number grew to ten they could get a synagogue, and Ephraim, the meek bill-collector, would be its priest. The little colony were happy in this hope, despite the abuse they received from Gentile neighbors, until the sickness fell upon Shushan. Confident in the protection of God, they defied the epidemic. But it took one and then another of the band, and the few who were untouched left sorrowfully for Calcutta.

JUDGMENT OF DUNGARA, THE. (*In Black and White.*) — A story of the vengeance which "the great God Dungara, the God of Things as They Are, executed on the converts of the Rev. Justus Krenk, pastor of the Tubingen Mission, and upon Lotta, his virtuous wife." The priest of Dungara hypocritically professed friendship and taught the Christian converts how to make clothes out of the fibre of a poisonous nettle. Soon after being put on, the garments stung unmercifully, and the superstitious natives leaped into the river, angrily renouncing together with their clothes the new religion of whose falsity Dungara had sent them so forcible a sign.

> "'The Judgment of Dungara,' with [its] rattling humor worthy of Lever." — *Gosse.*

JUDSON AND THE EMPIRE. (*Many Inventions.*) — Lieutenant Harrison Edward Judson, of the British Navy, commonly known as Bai-Jove Judson, interfered in the affairs of a little half-bankrupt European dependency in South Africa, and by the exercise of good-natured diplomacy "satisfied the self-love of a great and glorious people, and saved a monarchy from the ill-considered despotism which is called a Republic."

> "A very cheerful and entertaining story." — *Saturday Review.*

> "'Judson and the Empire,' in which Mr. Kipling breaks out in a new place, and annexes South Africa to the realms of his imagination, with a delicious disquisition on the Portuguese in his finest imperial manner." — *Athenæum.*

"JUST—SO" STORIES, THE. — Three fantastic children's

tales which appeared with illustrations in *St. Nicholas* for December, 1897 ; January, 1898 ; and February, 1898. They have never been included in any book of the author's.

KAA's HUNTING. (*Jungle Book.*) — Once, before Mowgli was turned out of the Wolf-pack, he got into trouble with the Bandar-log or Monkey people. Seizing the child, they bore him through lofty tree-tops to the Cold Lairs or Monkey City, and Baloo and Bagheera tried in vain to follow the captors. It was not until the aid of Kaa, the Rock Python, was enlisted that Mowgli's friends were equal to the task of rescuing him. The fight at the Lairs was a fearful one, but it ended successfully.

KIDNAPPED. (*Plain Tales.*) — A young English officer was determined on making an undesirable marriage which would have ruined his career. Mrs. Hauksbee saved him. Through her influence he obtained seven weeks' leave for a shooting-tour in Rajputana, whence he returned cured of his folly. All this shows the necessity of establishing "a properly conducted Matrimonial Department."

KING, THE. (*The Seven Seas.*) — Every age thinks that romance died with the age preceding. Yet the boy-god is with us still, revealing new wonders, as great as any of old, through steam and machinery. The "backward-gazing world" of to-day may not appreciate this, but the bard of to-morrow will.

KING's ANKUS, THE. (*Second Jungle Book.*) — Mowgli fights with and conquers White Hood, the treacherous cobra who guards the king's treasures. He carries away from the deserted vault a three-foot ankus (elephant goad) studded with jewels, but the snake warns him that it may kill him at last, for it is Death. When Mowgli grows tired

of its weight he throws it from him. A man finds it and
escapes. Mowgli and Bagheera, after following the trail,
discover that the ankus has been the cause of more than one
death among the covetous savages. Mowgli finally possesses himself of the jewelled goad, and returning to the
vault hurls it back among the treasure heaps. "Ah, ha !"
says the cobra. "It returns, then. I said the thing was
Death."

KITCHENER'S SCHOOL. — A ballad of ten stanzas, in the
London *Times*, Dec. 8, 1898, and in *Literature*, Dec.
10, 1898, beginning,

"Oh, Hubshee, carry your shoes in your hand and bow
your head on your breast ;
This is the message of Kitchener, who did not break you
in jest."

The poem purports to be "a translation of the song
that was made by a Mahomedan schoolmaster of the
Bengal Infantry (sometime on service at Suakim) when
he heard that the Sirdar was taking money from the English
to build a Madrissa for Hubshees — a college for the
Sudanese."

"The song is not Mr. Kipling at his best, but it is
very excellent rhymed journalism." — *Academy*.

LADIES, THE. (*The Seven Seas*.) — Tommy Atkins
recounts his various amours and bids us be warned by his
example. Incidentally he philosophizes knowingly on the
Sex.

LAMENT OF THE BORDER CATTLE THIEF, THE.
(*Ballads.*) — The rascal, now in jail "for lifting of the
kine," longs for his wild life again, and, wholly unrepent-
ant, threatens worse depredations if once he is liberated.

Lang Men o' Larut, The. (*Life's Handicap.*) —
Three enormously tall Scotchmen live in the tropical
dependency of Larut. Esdras B. Longer, of San Francisco,
himself six feet three, wagered a big drink, on first visiting
Larut, that he was the longest man on the island. The
bet was accepted and the three giants were successively
produced. It was not until Lang Lammitter, six feet
nine, was presented that the Californian collapsed. He
had meant to slide out of his bet, if he were overtopped, on
the strength of the riddle on his visiting-card. But in the
face of such total eclipse he could only stand treat for the
biggest drunk the island had ever known. This is one of
the shortest and poorest of Kipling's tales.

> "Unspeakably mediocre and wretched stuff." —
> *Francis Adams in Fortnightly.*

> See "The Wandering Jew."

Last Chantey, The. (*The Seven Seas.*) — After
Earth has passed away God decrees, on the petition of
"the silly sailor-folk," that the ocean remain undestroyed,
in order that

> "Such as have no pleasure
> For to praise the Lord by measure,
> They may enter into galleons and serve Him on the sea."

> "One of the purest examples since Coleridge's
> wondrous 'Rime' of the imaginatively grotesque." —
> *E. C. Stedman.*

Last Rhyme of True Thomas. (*The Seven Seas.*)
— An experiment in old ballad-form. In its archaic setting
it holds an eternal truth : the spiritual insight which belongs
to a seer or poet is greater than any material wealth or
power. True Thomas says scornfully to the king :

"I ha' harpit ye up to the Throne o' God,
   I ha' harpit your secret soul in three;
I ha' harpit ye down to the Hinges o' Hell,
   And—ye—would—make—a Knight o' me ! "

LAST SUTTEE, THE.   (*Ballads.*) — The story of a
queen who, disguised as the king's favorite dancing-girl,
sought death at the funeral pyre of her lord.

LAW OF THE JUNGLE, THE.   A poem following "How
Fear Came" in the *Second Jungle Book*.   It purports to
be a translation into verse of some of the laws applying to
the wolves.   The concluding couplet is:

"Now these are the Laws of the
   Jungle, and many and mighty are they;
But the head and the hoof of the
   Law and the haunch and the hump is — Obey ! "

LEGEND OF EVIL, THE.   (*Ballads.*) — A farcical poem
in two parts, explaining how the first monkeys who became
men were forced to leave off their friskiness and descend to
hard labor, and also how Noah unwittingly let the devil
into the ark at the same time with the donkey.

   "One of the most delightful bits of humorous verse
   in the language." — *Book Buyer.*

L'ENVOI (*to Barrack-Room Ballads*). — A lyric in
which the idea of a home voyage to England is employed
as the thread on which to string larger imaginative sugges-
tions.   It is richly musical, and the chorus has a rhythm
like that of waves.   There is, perhaps, an overplus of
nautical words.

L'ENVOI (*to Life's Handicap*). — One of the most
nobly devout of Kipling's poems.   A prayer to the "Great
Overseer."

" One instant's toil to Thee denied
Stands all eternity's offence."

L'Envoi (to *The Seven Seas*), beginning " When Earth's
last picture is painted, and the tubes are twisted and dried,"
is one of Kipling's finest lyrics. It embodies his healthy
gospel of work and furnishes more than one hint as to his
religious faith.

L'Envoi (to *The Story of The Gadsbys.*) — A poem
concluding the series of Gadsby stories and emphasizing
their somewhat cynical moral : A soldier married is a
soldier marred.

" White hands cling to the tightened rein,
Slipping the spur from the booted heel,
Tenderest voices cry, ' Turn again,'
Red lips tarnish the scabbarded steel,
High hopes faint on a warm hearthstone —
He travels the fastest who travels alone."

LETTERS OF MARQUE. (See *From Sea to Sea*.)

LETTING IN THE JUNGLE. (*Second Jungle Book.*) —
The villagers who had cast out Mowgli sent one of their
number to follow and kill this " devil-child." They also
determined to torture and burn to death Messua and her
husband. The boy easily escaped, but the rescue of his
reputed parents presented difficulties. Mowgli, however,
succeeded in putting them on their way to a town thirty
miles distant by jungle-trail. Then came the Revenge. It
was nothing less than a blotting-out of the village and a
driving-off of the inhabitants. Mowgli's four-footed allies,
led by Hathi, the elephant, carried out the work of de-
struction. By the end of the Rains the jungle covered the
spot that had been under plough a few months earlier.

" That fine poem of ' Letting in the Jungle ' . . .
is it not a drama of secular antagonism of nature and
man ? " — *Athenæum.*

" LIE STILL, LIE STILL ! O EARTH TO EARTH RETURN—
ING." — The first line of a poetical dialogue between the
pines of the Simla cemetery and the occupants of the
graves. (" Mrs. Hauksbee Sits Out.")

LIGHT THAT FAILED, THE. — (Published Philadelphia
and London, 1891.) Two orphan wards of a Pharisai-
cally-religious and sour-tempered woman (the counterpart of
" Aunty Rosa " in " Baa, Baa, Black Sheep ") were warmly
attached to one another in childhood — drawn together
by loneliness and by common defiance of their guardian's
tyranny. In a few years their paths separated. Dick became an artist and went to the Soudan with the Gordon
relief expedition to make illustrations for the English
papers. Maisie also studied art, and opened a studio in
London. On coming back to England, Dick brought with
him a well-earned reputation, an unconquerable love for the
girl, and a sword-cut on his head, received in action.
Maisie lacked talent, but thirsted for fame, and heartlessly
sacrificed Dick to her ambition. Dick's head-wound,
meanwhile, was seriously affecting the optic nerve ; he went
totally blind just as he had finished his masterpiece, Mel-
ancholia, " the likeness of a woman who had known all
the sorrow in the world and was laughing at it." But
Bessie Broke, the model who had posed for him, vindic-
tively ruined the canvas and ran off with her liberal pay, in
revenge for Dick's interference in her love-affair with Torpenhow, a war correspondent, whose acquaintance he had
made in the East. Maisie, who was now once more
studying in Paris, was informed by Torpenhow of Dick's

blindness, but she proved more unwilling than ever to devote herself to him.   Dick, heart-broken, went again to the Soudan, where fighting was in progress between British and native troops, and, seated on a camel, insisted on being placed in the front of the fighting-line.   A welcome bullet ended his life.   In the *Lippincott Magazine* version, Maisie proves faithful to Dick, and the story ends happily. The present dénouement, however, is the more logical, and the one preferred by Mr. Kipling, who prefaces the book with the statement : " This is the story of *The Light that Failed* as it was originally conceived by the writer."   The novel has powerful passages, and some of its descriptions are in Kipling's strongest manner, but it lacks interesting and vigorous characterization, and is too uniformly depressing.   It cannot be reckoned among his masterpieces.

" A very uneven book ; the parts, especially the campaigning scenes, are infinitely better than the whole. But a work which displays the same graphic power of presentation, the same condensed vigor, the same liveliness of narrative, that characterized the slighter sketches, is necessarily of no ordinary kind.   The canvas is larger ; it is filled with more figures ; its background is more extended.   But none of the work is slurred or shirked.   It is firm, clear, and strong. . . . On the other hand, the book exhibits a fault to which Mr. Kipling is always inclined.   It is needlessly hard and gratuitously brutal." — *Edinburgh Review*, 1891.

" It is hardly a story so much as a succession of scenes and conversations, mostly among press men and newspaper correspondents, who talk entirely in slang of the most audacious type, and seems to have been intended partly as a vehicle for conveying the writer's opinions on art and society, for it is pretty evident that the hero of the story is to a great extent the author's mouthpiece. There are brilliant pages in it, but we should say that little trouble went to the writing of it, and that it is flung together rather than composed." — *Edinburgh Review*, 1898.

" Although *The Light that Failed* runs only to a volume, it is one of those novels which threaten to break down at the end of every chapter. It has few personages, and its incidents may be reckoned on the fingers of one hand. Take away the conversations which do not help on the story, and it would shrink to less than a hundred pages. . . . *The Light that Failed* is a dish of highly-seasoned fragments, served up with a deal of sarcastic commentary on life as it is lived in Bohemia." — *Quarterly*.

" *The Light that Failed* is an organic whole — a book with a backbone — and stands out boldly among the nerveless, flaccid, invertebrate things called novels that enjoy an expensive but ephemeral existence in the circulating libraries." — *Athenæum*.

For a severe and extended criticism of *The Light that Failed* see *Mr. Kipling's Stories*, J. M. Barrie, *Contemporary Review*, March, 1891.

LIMITATIONS OF PAMBÉ SERANG. (*Life's Handicap.*)— A Zanzibar stoker, when in drink, did an injury to Pambé, a Malay employed on the same steamer. The latter refused to accept the apology of the negro, and lived with the one thought of revenge. From country to country Pambé tracked his enemy until finally the former fell ill in London. While still in his bed he recognized Nurkeed's voice in the street and induced the missionary seated beside him to call the negro in. The latter, when leaning over the sick man, received a knife-thrust under the edge of his rib bone.   Pambé recovered sufficiently to be hanged.

" Liner She's a Lady, The.''   (*The Seven Seas.*) — While the Liner has the Man-o'-War for husband, and proves her ladyhood "by the paint upon 'er face,'' the little cargo-boats which have "to load or die " are England's pride and the source of her "'ome an' foreign trade.''

Lispeth.   (*Plain Tales.*) — Illustrates the truth that a mere dab of Christianity is insufficient to " wipe out uncivilized Eastern instincts.''   Lispeth, a beautiful hill girl, grows to womanhood in a Christian mission.   But she meets and falls violently in love with a visiting Britisher whose flirtation she takes to be a serious expression of love. When he leaves he promises to return and marry her, and the missionary, hoping thus to quiet her, encourages the deception.   The girl, on finally learning that she has been played with, loses all faith in the new religion and modes of life, and returns to her mother's gods and the degraded habits of her caste.

Little Tobrah.   (*Life's Handicap.*) — The smallpox struck little Tobrah's village, took away his parents, and left the sister blind.   The small property left the three children was soon lost.   A famine rose, the older brother deserted them, and the young boy and girl were unable to get food.   Finally, on coming to a well, Tobrah thrust his sister in, believing it " better to die than to starve.''   On the discovery of the dead body little Tobrah was brought to trial, but since there were no witnesses he was acquitted.

Loot.   (*Ballads.*) — A frank expression of opinion by Tommy Atkins.   He wholly fails to understand

" Why lootin' should be entered as a crime.
So if my song you'll 'ear, I will learn you plain an' clear
'Ow to pay yourself for fightin' overtime.''

LOST LEGION, THE.   (*Many Inventions.*) — It is not
easy to manage one ghost, as any story-writer will admit,
but to write of a whole ghostly regiment would overtax the
powers of any living man of genius except Mr. Kipling.
Even in his hands it would be merely grotesque were it
not so carefully subordinated to the blood-and-flesh main
plot, which relates to the capture by a frontier force of
British of a notorious Afghan outlaw with thirteen brother
murderers.   The story of the secret journey by night to
the latter's lair in the hills is admirably told.

"Mr. Kipling's best war-piece.'' — *Blackwoods.*
" A splendid ghost story.'' — *Academy.*

LOST LEGION, THE.   (*Ballads.*) — A rollicking song
of the "Gentlemen Rovers " — a "Legion that never
was 'listed.''

"LOVE–O'–WOMEN.''   (*Many Inventions.*) — Larry
Tighe, nicknamed Love-o'-Women, was a handsome man
when Mulvaney first knew him, but "wicked as all hell.''
His favorite amusement was that of seducing innocent
women.   When next they met, Love-'o-Women was suf-
fering damning tortures of remorse.   The faces of his victims rose before him to make his nights sleepless and his
days insufferable.   But the crown of his punishment was
the memory of one woman whom he might have loved, but
whom he had ruined and cast away.   The dramatic ending of the tale makes the man discover this former sweetheart and die in her arms.   She completes the tragedy by
committing suicide.

" Perhaps the most powerful story in the book is the one called ' Love-o'-Women.' As a picture of true remorse it is most impressive. . . . It certainly shows Mr. Kipling at his highest point of literary power." — *Spectator.*

" The best of them all [*i.e.*, stories in *Many Inventions*], to our mind, is ' Love-o'-Women,' which is, indeed, one of the most masterly things its author has yet done. . . . It is worth a hundred addresses on Social Purity platforms ; and yet it is written with an artistic reticence which is beyond all praise." — *Athenæum.*

LUKANNON. — A poem of six stanzas following " The White Seal " in the *Jungle Book.* It is " a sort of very sad seal national anthem," ending with the line :   •
" The beaches of Lukannon shall know their sons no more."

MADNESS OF PRIVATE ORTHERIS, THE. (*Plain Tales.*) — Ortheris becomes homesick for London, " sick for the sounds of 'er, an' the sights of 'er, and the stinks of 'er." He questions, " Wot's the good of sodjerin'," and goes so far as to don citizen's clothes and attempt desertion. By the time dusk shuts down, however, Ortheris has returned penitently to his companions. His loneliness, the strangeness of his garb, and the force of the old habits, have cured his madness.

MALTESE CAT, THE. (*Day's Work.*) — The story of a polo-pony whose intelligence and quickness won the great game between the Archangels and the Skidars. The description of the contest is exceedingly spirited. As in " Her Majesty's Servants " and " A Walking Delegate," we are regaled with the conversation of horses.

" It goes splendidly, and entitles its author to rank with the very small band who have described athletic games in progress without losing most of their thrill and movement." — *Athenæum*.

" ' The Maltese Cat,' that delightful polo story (every polo player should know it by heart) where the animals give us their version of the game." — *Academy*.

" Something rather better than excellent descriptive journalism." — *Spectator*.

MAN WHO WAS, THE.   (*Life's Handicap.*) — A former officer in the White Hussars, who has been for thirty years a Russian captive, escapes from Siberia and succeeds in discovering his regiment.   The limp heap of rags is crawling past the sentries, when he is shot at for a carbine-thief. Brought in through a mistake to the mess-table, where the officers are entertaining a Russian guest, and toasting Her Majesty, he exhibits his shrinking dread of the Cossack, his undying loyalty to the Queen, and awful evidence of his tortures.   The wretched man dies shortly after.

" For pathos rising into tragedy and as curious, strange, and unexpected as it is touching, choose ' The Man who Was.' " — *Boston Transcript*.

" That glorious masterpiece, ' The Man who Was.' " — *Gentleman's Magazine*.

" ' The Man who Was,' an admirable story, full of that indefinable spirit, military patriotism, and regimental pride." — *Academy*.

MAN WHO WOULD BE KING, THE.   (*Phantom 'Rickshaw, etc.*) — Two shrewd adventurers, Daniel Dravot and Peachey Carnehan, decide that India isn't large enough for them, and aspire to become rulers of Kafristan. Disguised as a mad priest, Dravot, taking Carnehan with him as a servant, makes his way safely to the prospective kingdom. Dravot gains unlimited power over the native tribes, who think him a god and give him a gold crown. Another is made for his companion, and they rule their new empire jointly. Finally Dravot blunders by demanding a wife. The wench allotted to him puts his godhood to test by biting him. On seeing his blood the people pronounce him an impostor, subject him to a cruel death and Carnehan to fearful tortures. The latter, wrecked in body and mind, lives to reach India, carrying the head of Dravot in a bag.

A number of eminent literary men in an informal gathering " resolved to write out, each for himself, a list of the best half-dozen of Mr. Kipling's short stories," so Mr. S. R. Crockett has informed the readers of the *Bookman*. ' The papers were folded. They were put into the hat. . . . ' The Man who would be King ' stood proudly at the head of every list."

" For ' The Man who would be King,' our author's masterpiece, there is no word but magnificent. . . . Positively, it is the most audacious thing in fiction, and yet it reads as true as *Robinson Crusoe.* " — *J. M. Barrie.*

MANDALAY. (*Ballads.*) — A British soldier, now in London, hears " the East a-callin'," and grows homesick for the familiar sights and sounds on the road to Mandalay.

" For the wind is in the palm-trees, and the temple-bells they say,

' Come you back, you British soldier; come you back to Mandalay ! ' "

This is probably Kipling's most widely known ballad.

"A work of very high art indeed." — *Saturday Review.*

"A wonderful song of the fascination of the East." — *Edinburgh Review.*

MARK OF THE BEAST, THE. (*Life's Handicap.*) — Fleete, an Englishman, grossly insulted a native idol in its temple. Whereupon a hideous, faceless leper employed in the service of the god sprang out at the man, and catching him about the body, dropped his head on the victim's breast. The terrible disease that overtook the latter in consequence seemed not to be leprosy, but a madness more awful than hydrophobia, though closely resembling it. Its growth, symptoms, and final cure are described with terrible power. For pure horror, this tale is, perhaps, unmatched in English literature.

"In 'The Mark of the Beast' Mr. Kipling passes, as he occasionally does, the bounds of decorum, and displays a love of the crudely horrible in its disgusting details . . . which is to be deprecated ; but the fascination of the story is incontestable." — *Athenæum.*

"'The Mark of the Beast' may be curious, but is also loathsome, and shows Mr. Kipling at his very worst." — *Spectator.*

"As a tale of sheer terror, 'The Mark of the Beast' could not easily be surpassed." — *Pall Mall Gazette.*

MARY GLOSTER, THE. (*The Seven Seas.*) — A disagreeable but intensely real character study. Sir Anthony Gloster, Philistine and millionaire ship-owner, holds conversation on his death-bed with his only son, Dickie. The old man reveals both his ingrained vulgarity and also his complete incapacity to appreciate his son's artistic and literary tastes, which are to the Baronet merely "whims" and "sick fancies."

" ' The Mary Gloster,' though somewhat too *risqué virginibus puerisque*, is a piece of rare power." — *Henry Austin in Dial.*

MARY, PITY WOMEN !   (*The Seven Seas.*)— A bitter protest addressed to a faithless lover by the woman whom he has ruined.

MATTER OF FACT, A.   (*Many Inventions.*) — Three newspaper men, an American, a Dutchman, and the author, were the only passengers on a little tramp steamer.   When in mid-ocean they had a narrow escape from wreck by reason of a tidal wave thrown up by a volcano.   In the resulting commotion, a great sea-serpent came to the surface to die, and, as the carcass sank, the loathsome mate swam round and round it, and disappeared.   The American, on recovering his nerve, was for cabling this biggest scoop on record to the New York *World.*   He was dissuaded by the Englishman, who wished to appropriate it to his own use as fiction.   This sketch contains some sharp satire on American journalism, but is chiefly notable for its almost Shakespearian description of the serpent's death.

" An astonishing story. . . . Perfectly successful and convincing." — *Academy.*

" To our mind the most striking of the new tales in the present volume." — *Saturday Review (in review of Many Inventions, June* 17, 1893).

" Almost worthy of Poe." — *Critic.*

McANDREW'S HYMN.   (*The Seven Seas.*) — Wherein we are shown the heart of a Scotch engineer, employed on a big passenger steamship.   He's a good Calvinist, but very human.   And his sincerest passion is for his engines.   One feels that McAndrew echoes Mr. Kipling's own feelings when he exclaims :

"Lord, send a man like Robbie Burns to sing the 'Song o' Steam' ! "

> "It is too lengthy and too carelessly written to hold its ground as poetry." — *Edinburgh Review.*
>
> "A poem of surpassing excellence alike in conception and in execution." — *C. E. Norton in Atlantic.*

MEN THAT FOUGHT AT MINDEN, THE. (*The Seven Seas.*) — A song of instruction for the benefit of green recruits.

MERCHANTMEN, THE. (*The Seven Seas.*) — A song of London "sailormen" who are bringing back to port a cargo gathered "with sweat and aching bones." They have been abroad on all seas, and relate wonderful experiences.

> "Mr. Kipling is at his best in a long poem with a strong subject. 'The Merchantmen' is among his best ; so is 'Mulholland's Contract.'" — *Academy.*

MIRACLE OF PURUN BHAGAT, THE. (*Second Jungle Book.*) — A high-caste Brahmin, with university degrees, renounced wealth and office to become a barefoot "holy man" carrying a begging bowl. As the mendicant crossed an Himalayan pass he came upon a deserted shrine. "Here shall I find peace," he said. Immediately below him the hillside fell away for 1,500 feet, and in the valley huddled a village of stone-walled houses. His days and nights of contemplation, shared only by wild animals who grew boldly familiar, were finally disturbed by a landslide resulting from the heavy rains. He succeeded, just in time, in warning the villagers of their danger. The manner in which the hermit had accomplished their rescue seemed to the village folk miraculous, and on his death, which followed from exhaustion, they built a temple to mark his grave.

MIRACLES, THE. (*The Seven Seas.*) — In this remarkable little poem the miracles of modern science — cable, telegraph, steam locomotive, etc. — are very imaginatively conceived and celebrated.

MISS YOUGHAL'S SAIS. (*Plain Tales.*) — When Strickland, the Sherlock Holmes of Kipling's stories, asked Miss Youghal's hand in marriage, her parents refused consent. The lover, used to many disguises, got himself up as a native servant, and became "attached to Miss Youghal's Arab." He preserved the incognito for months. Finally when a certain general who had taken the young lady for a ride persisted in a disagreeable flirtation, Strickland lost patience and in the most fluent English threatened the offender with punishment. When the officer had learned the truth he saw the humor of the situation and pledged the couple his assistance. Through his influence the reluctant consent of the girl's parents was obtained, and the story ends happily.

MORNING-SONG IN THE JUNGLE. — A poem beginning:

> "One moment past our bodies cast
> No shadow on the plain."

It occurs in "Letting in the Jungle" (*Second Jungle Book*), and is a rendering into English verse of a song sung by the wolves.

MOTHER O' MINE, O MOTHER O' MINE! — The refrain of the striking verse-dedication of *The Light that Failed*.

MOTHER-LODGE, THE. (*The Seven Seas.*) — The singer longs for another sight of his Mother Lodge, where his "Brethren black an' brown" — men of all faiths and of every rank — "met upon the Level an' parted on the Square."

MOTI GUJ — MUTINEER. (*Life's Handicap.*) — Moti Guj was the elephant and drunken Deesa was the owner. They quarrelled, but they loved each other, and when Deesa told the elephant that he would be gone for ten days and that Chihun would be his master meanwhile the beast submitted with manifest reluctance. On the eleventh morning, when Deesa failed to come according to promise, Moti Guj mutinied, refusing to work, chasing an English planter, and showing fight generally. The story proceeds to describe the elephant's vain search for his lord, and the great joy of both at meeting again, when Deesa, who had been gorgeously drunk, finally returned.

> "Except in its sardonic form, humor has never been a prominent feature of Mr. Kipling's prose. I hardly know of an instance of it not disturbed by irony or savagery, except the story of 'Moti Guj.'"—*Edmund Gosse, Century*, 1891.

MOWGLI'S BROTHERS. (*Jungle Book*). — A naked brown baby, lost in the jungle, is rescued by a wolf from the jaws of Shere Khan, the tiger. The man-cub is borne to a cave, and there suckled and cared for by Mother Wolf and given the name Mowgli, or the Frog. After much discussion, Mowgli is adopted into the Pack and is allowed to run with them and to share their life unharmed. Besides the wolves, he has for friends Baloo, the brown bear, and Bagheera, the panther. But Shere Khan remains his sworn enemy. When Mowgli has grown to boyhood the tiger's plot against his life is foiled through the lad's boldness and presence of mind, but he is forced to leave the Pack and to seek a dwelling among men.

MOWGLI'S SONG. — This is the song that Mowgli sang at the council rock when he danced on Shere Khan's hide.

It is written in irregular unrhymed lines, and follows "Tiger! Tiger!" in the *Jungle Book*.

MOWGLI'S SONG AGAINST PEOPLE. — A five stanza poem which follows "Letting in the Jungle" in the *Second Jungle Book*.

MRS. HAUKSBEE SITS OUT. — (Added to *Under the Deodars* in the *Outward Bound* edition.) A dramatic sketch, scene laid in Simla, with the subtitle, "An Unhistorical Extravaganza." Miss May Holt, assisted by Mrs. Hauksbee, eludes the vigilance of a Puritanic aunt and attends a volunteer ball. Here she meets her lover, a young lieutenant. The aunt follows, furious, but is at length subdued at the hands of the enemy, now reënforced by an Irish major who drags her, scandalized, into the waltz, and by the Viceroy of India (in Mrs. Hauksbee's confidence), who affects interest in the good lady's missionary schemes. Finally May's lover himself plays a successful part in the taming of the shrew, and the comedy ends propitiously.

MULHOLLAND'S CONTRACT. (*The Seven Seas.*) — A deck-hand on a cattle-boat, when in imminent danger of death, made a contract with God that if He would save his life, he for his part would reform and "praise his Holy Majesty till further orders came." The sailor's life was spared, and acting in accordance with a special revelation, he returned to the cattle-boats and preached the gospel there. He writes of his experience as an evangelist.

"As profound as it is simple."—*Academy.*

See, also, "The Merchantmen."

MUTINY OF THE MAVERICKS, THE. (*Life's Handicap.*) — A Fenian organization in America sent young Mulcahy to

India to spread sedition in an Irish regiment. The
"Mavericks," who were perversely loyal to the Queen,
although willing to impress Mulcahy with their sympathy
in order to enjoy the unlimited beer he furnished, were in
reality glad when a chance for action gave them an excuse
for pressing the unwilling recruit into the front of the battle
line.   From excessive cowardice he passed into a mood of
mad bravery, and rushing into the enemy's ranks died on
an Afghan knife.

> "'The Mutiny of the Mavericks' and 'Namgay
> Doola' are pure comedy.   .   .   .   Charmingly good-
> natured satires upon the inhabitants of the sister isle. —
> *Athenæum*.

"MY GIRL SHE GIVE ME THE GO ONST." — First line of
the song sung by Ortheris in "The Courting of Dinah
Shadd" (*q.v.*).

MY LORD THE ELEPHANT. (*Many Inventions.*) —
When a young man in Cawnpore Mulvaney tamed a
furious elephant that had been terrorizing the streets and
playing havoc with a carriage shop.   Filled with whiskey
and bravado, he took a mad ride on the back of "Ould
Double Ends," but beat him at last into submission.
Years afterwards, when one of the gun-elephants, who
proves to be our former acquaintance, refused to trust a
troop-bridge near the head of the Tangi Pass and kept an
impatient army waiting on his pleasure, Mulvaney left a
hospital cot and came to the rescue.   The Cawnpore elephant recognized his old tamer and responded to his urging.

> "Perhaps the best story in the book" [*i.e., Many
> Inventions*]. — *Spectator*.

> "'My Lord the Elephant' is pure, unadulterated
> farce.   In this most flamboyant, most coruscating of

yarns, Mulvaney comes near to beating (and it is much to say) the record of his famous ' Incarnation.' His ride on the infuriated tusker is as fine as that of Tam o' Shanter himself." — *Athenæum*.

MY OWN TRUE GHOST STORY. (*Phantom 'Rickshaw, etc.*) — The author passed a night in a dirty little dâk-bungalow. After the usual ghost-story overtures of rattling curtains and lamps throwing quaint shadows, there came the sound of a game of billiards in the room adjoining. Now, this room was not large enough to hold a billiard-table, but in the morning it was discovered that the three small rooms of the dâk-bungalow had once been a single apartment which was used as a billiard-room, and that (according to the servant) a Sahib had died · there while playing the game. Here surely was a juicy morsel for the Psychical Research Society. But disillusion followed, and a good mystery was spoiled by a very simple discovery.

MY SUNDAY AT HOME. (*Day's Work.*) — A guard called out at each compartment of an English railway train : '' Has any gentleman here a bottle of medicine ? A gentleman has taken a bottle of laudanum by mistake.'' By *taken* he meant *carried off*, but an officious American doctor, supposing that some passenger had swallowed the poison, rushed up to a very drunk and boisterous '' navvy '' in a rear compartment, dragged him upon the platform of the station where the train was stopping, and dosed him heavily with an emetic. The results were highly ludicrous, not to say tragic.

'' A hash of fantastic effects, partially redeemed from extravagance by the excellence of the character drawing.'' — *London Daily News*.

NABOTH.   (*Life's Handicap.*) — A modern version of
Naboth's vineyard from the point of view of Ahab, and incidentally "an allegory of empire." Naboth was a native
who began his acquaintance with the author by begging.
The "Protector of the Poor" gave him a rupee, whereupon Naboth craved the privilege of selling sweetmeats
near the house of his benefactor. It was granted, and the
tale deals with the prosperous dependent's successive in-
roads on the shrubbery of the Sahib. Finally, Naboth,
with his mud hut surrounded by bamboo network, was
banished. The summer-house which took the place of
Naboth's hut resembled a fort on the author's frontier,
whence he thereafter guarded his kingdom.

NAMGAY DOOLA.   (*Life's Handicap.*) — In a little
native kingdom in the Himalayas there was one subject who
refused to pay taxes, and had an unpleasant way of breaking the heads of all who interfered with him. The king,
pondering on the best punishment, asked the counsel of the
author. The latter, on learning that this red-haired rebel
was the son of Thimla Dhula (Tim Doolan) by a native
wife, advised the king to raise him to a position of honor in
the army, since he came of a race which would not.pay
revenue, but which, if filled with words and favor, would
work heroically. The advice was followed with successful
results.

See " The Mutiny of the Mavericks."

[1] NATIVE-BORN, THE.   (*The Seven Seas.*) — A magnificent tribute to imperial Britain —

" To the last and the largest Empire,
To the map that is half unrolled."

---

[1] By "the Native-born " is meant the man of English ancestry
who is born outside of England.

The spirit and dash of the final chorus, beginning

"A health to the Native-born (Stand up !)
    We're six white men a-row,"

are inimitable.

NAULAHKA, THE : A STORY OF WEST AND EAST. [Collaborated with Wolcott Balestier. Appeared serially in *Century Magazine.* Published, Heinemann, 1892 ; Macmillan, 1892. The title (pronounced Now-làh-ka, —see *Critic,* Nov. 14, 1891) means the nine-lakh-er, that is to say, the thing worth nine lakhs, the very precious one. " Nine lakhs of rupees would be £90,000, if the rupee were worth two shillings, as it used to be three decades ago." — London *Literary World,* quoted in *Literary News,* September, 1892.] Nicholas Tarvin is a hustling Western man with two objects in life. One is to win the hand of a girl who has rejected him in order to devote herself to Zenana mission work. The other is to make his town, Topaz, Col., a railroad centre. In order to bring about the latter end he gains an influence over the young wife of the President of the " Three C.'s," — the railroad he hopes may be run to Topaz instead of finding its terminus at the rival town of Rustler, fifteen miles off, — and, discovering jewelry to be the woman's secret passion, he promises to fetch her from Rajputana the priceless necklace, "Naulahka," in return for her influence with her husband in behalf of his scheme. She consents. Tarvin leaves for India with his double prize in view, and arrives at Rhatore before Kate Sheriff, his recalcitrant sweetheart, who almost cries with vexation when she discovers that even half the earth's circumference fails to rid her of his importunities. The rest of the story is devoted to the young man's determined effort to attain the necklace and to win the consent of Kate.   After superhuman courage and endurance and the undergoing of enough hairbreadth escapes to satisfy any adventurous boy he succeeds in both objects.   The girl, discouraged at last by the break-down of her hospital, into which she has put tireless work and interest, yields to the man's solicitations.   The Naulahka, in deference to Kate's sensitive notions of honor, is returned to its owner, after a terrible struggle on the part of Tarvin.   When it becomes clear to him that he must choose between the woman he loves and the consummation of a selfish purpose he hesitates no longer, but sacrifices one of his two great ambitions to the other, and returns to America with his bride.   The interest of the story is not in the character-drawing, which is in the main unreal and featureless, nor in the double plot, which is somewhat confusing and ill-joined, nor in the style, which lacks the distinction of Kipling's best work.   The interest is episodical. It is in the descriptions of audacious intrigues, of amazing adventures, of Oriental mysteries, of the secrets of the Royal Zenana, — descriptions of the midnight ride when the American meets the bewitching and cruel Gypsy Queen, of the plots against the young prince's life, of Tarvin's escape from the murderous assault of the gray ape, of the ride to the deserted city.   These wonders may tax credulity, but they inevitably hold the attention.   Perhaps, after all, the most distinguishing excellence of the novel lies in the penetration with which Mr. Kipling gets behind the native consciousness and reveals all its odd workings.   For while lacking in well-developed studies of character, the story dazzles us with occasional flashes of marvellous intuition. The first four chapters, devoted to America, are only indifferently good, but as soon as India is reached the hand of Kipling becomes more apparent than that of his collaborator, and the East is made actually to live before us.

" A story which brings into sudden and glaring contrast the impenetrable, unchanging barbarism of the East and the bran-new civilization of the West, hardly less barbaric, less reckless, or less corrupt. . . . It seems to us that collaboration is to Mr. Kipling very much what the admixture of water is to champagne."
— *Westminster Review.*

" Why should Mr. Kipling hamper himself with a partner? We like him best alone. . . . There is no one but Mr. Kipling who can make his readers taste and smell as well as see and hear the East; and in this book . . . he has surely surpassed himself."
— *Athenæum.*

" *The Naulahka* falls far below the standard of Mr. Kipling's general work. . . . One cannot help remarking how strangely wanting the story is in Mr. Kipling's ordinary conciseness, strength of diction, and directness of purpose. . . . *The Naulahka* is not a well-told story — we might even say it is told extremely ill. There is a want of unity in its design, and of smoothness in its progress. . . . The plot is not a good one. The twofold motive of Tarvin's pilgrimage to India confounds the sympathy of the reader, who is never quite sure whether it is the Naulahka . . . or the love of Kate which is uppermost in the hero's mind. Tarvin himself confounds all sense of probability. . . . There are good passages in the book. Every now and then we are glad to recognize Mr. Kipling's great descriptive powers,

. . . but these purple patches are few and far between." — *Spectator*.

OF THOSE CALLED. (*Soldiers Three.*) — A story told on steamer-board during a heavy fog, regarding the loss, during just such a fog, of a lumbering "tramp" which was rammed by an English iron-clad. Three half-drowned survivors were rescued by means of a rope thrown them from the man-of-war. About half an hour later the fog lifted.

ON GREENHOW HILL. (*Life's Handicap.*) — Learoyd, the Yorkshireman, relates the romance of his early life. When climbing a stone wall he has fallen and broken his arm. Carried to a neighboring house, he is nursed by the daughter of the family, 'Liza Roantree, with whom he falls in love. He is influenced to renounce his rough life and to join the Primitive Methodists, of which sect 'Liza is a member. He becomes jealous of the chapel minister, who also loves 'Liza. But Death foils both lovers ; after a rapid decline the girl dies. Before her death Learoyd learns that he would have been the favored suitor. He goes at once into the army, and has been trying to forget her ever since.

"One of Kipling's very best efforts." — *National Observer*.

For a more conservative estimate, see Mr. Gosse's article in the *Century*, 1891.

ON THE CITY WALL. (*In Black and White.*) — An Oriental Delilah has a house upon the east wall of a city in India. The author (or narrator, writing in the first person) is drawn into the pretty creature's toils, and becomes her tool in helping an important political prisoner, who has taken refuge in her apartments, to escape from the town, on the occasion of a great riot between Hindus and Mussulmen in the city streets. The marvellous description of this riot, the picture of Lalun's beauty and fascination, and the analysis of the character of Wali Dad, the youthful cynic, once a Mohammedan but now a " Demnition Product," whom the riot sweeps back into the fanatical current of the faith once abandoned, unite to make this story one of extraordinary interest and power.

> " A masterpiece." — *Quarterly*.
> See " At Twenty-two."

On the Strength of a Likeness. (*Plain Tales.*) — A youth who had cherished an unrequited attachment, became devoted to another woman, simply, as he thought, on the strength of her remarkable likeness to his lost sweetheart. He found out too late that he had come to worship her for her own qualities.

One View of the Question. (*Many Inventions.*) — A high-caste Mussulman writes a long letter to an intimate in India describing life in London, where he has gone on a commission for His Highness the Rao Sahib of Jagesur. English life is looked at from a severely Oriental point of view. " This town, London, which is as large as all Jagesur, is accursed, being dark and unclean, devoid of sun, and full of low-born, who are perpetually drunk, and howl in the streets like jackals, men and women together." The Government is scored, on various grounds, with Gulliverian satire.

> " An exceedingly, strong, thoughtful, and interesting satire." — *Saturday Review*.

Only a Subaltern. (*Under the Deodars.*) — Bobby Wicks, the apple of his father's eye, had not long been a member of the Tail Twisters before proving himself one of the most popular men in the regiment. When the cholera struck the camp he was unremitting in his services to the men, especially to old private Dormer, a dirty, drunken fellow, whose one virtue was his love for Bobby. As a result of over-exposure in caring for Dormer, the boy was finally stricken down himself, and after three days' struggle died.

> "*Under the Deodars* has one redeeming feature — the excellent story called 'Only a Subaltern,' with which it concludes. We have read nothing of the kind so good since Mrs. Ewing's *Jackanapes*." — *Athenæum*.

OONTS. (*Ballads.*) — Mr. Atkins gives his opinion as to the merits and defects of the camel, or oont :

" The 'orse 'e knows above a bit, the bullock's but a fool,
The elephant's a gentleman, the battery-mule's a mule ;
But the commissariat cam-u-el, when all is said an' done,
'E's a devil an' a' ostrich an' a' orphan child in one."

OTHER MAN, THE. (*Plain Tales.*) — A girl, in love with a young officer without a fortune, was married by her parents to a rich old colonel. The Other Man, transferred to an unhealthful station, became ill. The woman's heart, not at all with her husband, who neglected her, was still with the Other Man. Finally the latter was sent up from his station on a chance of recovery. The colonel's wife went to meet him. When she found him he was seated on the back seat of his " tonga " — dead. The long up-hill jolt had been too much for his weak heart-valve. The sequel is even more tragic.

See " At the Pit's Mouth."

OUR LADY OF THE SNOWS. (*i.e.*, *Canada.*) — A poem of six stanzas contributed to the London *Times* and written after the publication of Laurier's new tariff bill in

May, 1897. It takes as its text : " Last, but not least (he said), we give to the people the benefits of preferential trade with the mother-country." — *New Canadian Tariff.* The poem was quoted in the *Critic,* May 15, 1897.

> " A nation spoke to a nation,
>> A queen sent word to a throne :
> Daughter am I in my mother's house,
>> But mistress in my own.
> The gates are mine to open
>> As the gates are mine to close,
> And I set my house in order,
>> Said the Lady of the Snows."

" OUR LITTLE MAID THAT HATH NO BREASTS." — First line of the " Queen's Song from Libretto of Naulahka," a striking poem prefixed to Chapter Twenty of *The Naulahka.*

OUT OF INDIA. (See Bibliography of First Editions.) In the *Critic* for Nov. 9, 1895, occurs this " Card from Mr. Kipling " :

" *To the Editors of the Critic :*

" Will you permit me through the medium of your columns to warn the public against a book called ' Out of India,' recently published by a New York firm ? It is put forward evidently as a new book by Rudyard Kipling. It is made up of a hash of old newspaper articles written nine or ten years ago, to which are added moral reflections by some unknown hand. It appears, of course, without my knowledge or sanction, is a common ' fake,' and I must disclaim all connection with it.

" RUDYARD KIPLING.

" WAITE, VT., 3 Nov., 1895."

OUTSONG, THE. (*Second Jungle Book.*) — A poem

following " The Spring Running " in the *Second Jungle Book*. It is " the song that Mowgli heard behind him in the jungle till he came to Messua's door again." Part of this farewell song is uttered by Baloo, part by Kaa, part by Bagheera, part by all three. The refrain is : " Jungle-Favor go with thee ! "

OVER THE EDGE OF THE PURPLE DOWN. — The first line of " the Brushwood girl's " song. (See " The Brushwood Boy," *The Day's Work.*)

PARADE–SONG OF THE CAMP ANIMALS. — A poem following " Her Majesty's Servants " in the *Jungle Book*. Elephants of the Gun Team, Gun Bullocks, Cavalry Horses, Screw-Gun Mules, and Commissariat Camels, all bear a part, and the final chorus, " Children of the Camp are we," etc., is sung by all the beasts together.

PHANTOM 'RICKSHAW, THE. (*The Phantom 'Rickshaw and Other Tales.*) — A man who has heartlessly jilted a faithful woman and has brutally repulsed all her pitiful appeals for kindness is pursued, after she dies, by her ghost. Wherever he goes the apparition of the woman whom he has killed, seated in her accustomed 'rickshaw, awaits him with the old-time pleadings and remonstrances. His death, attributed by his physicians to overwork, is in reality the result of this strange persecution. This excursion into the occult, while cleverly enough managed, lacks the originality of Kipling's best stories.

> " Kipling's deliberately supernatural tales, from 'The Phantom 'Rickshaw' downwards, impress me as distinct failures." — *Francis Adams in Fortnightly.*
>
> The *Edinburgh Review* (1891) objected to this tale, with " its abrupt intrusion into every-day life of a crudely material supernaturalism."

"Guy de Maupassant himself has hardly surpassed 'The Phantom 'Rickshaw,' by which I have been more moved and haunted than by any other of Kipling's stories." — *Louise Chandler Moulton.*

PHARAOH AND THE SERGEANT. — A poem of seven stanzas contributed to *McClure's* for September, 1897, beginning :

"Said England unto Pharaoh, ' I must make a man of you
That will stand upon his feet and play the game ;
That will Maxim his oppressor as a Christian ought to do.'
And she sent old Pharaoh Sergeant Whatisname."

PIG. (*Plain Tales.*) — Pinecoffin cheated Nafferton in a horse-trade. Nafferton determined to get even. He informed the Government that he had a scheme for feeding a large percentage of the British army in India, at a great saving, on pig, and he hinted that Pinecoffin (who was in the Civil Service) might supply him with the necessary facts. This was ordered, and Pinecoffin was trapped into a voluminous correspondence. Nafferton, making use of some parts and suppressing others, found plausible support for his complaint of inadequate assistance. Government and press united in censuring Pinecoffin.

PIT THAT THEY DIGGED, THE. (*Under the Deodars.*) — An amusing story of official red tape. A member of the Bengal Civil Service lay down to die of fever ; doctors gave him up for lost. The Government "prepared, according to regulation, a brick-lined grave." But on the man's sudden recovery the question rose, " Who pays the bill ? " The yearly accounts were made up ; and there remained over, unpaid for, one grave ; cost, one hundred and seventy-five rupees fourteen annas. The vouchers for all the other graves carried the name of a deceased servant of the Government. A complicated and lengthy correspondence followed among departments and commissions. Finally the question was unwittingly settled by the resurrected man himself. He died, the entry was passed to "regular account," and " there was peace in India."

PRIVATE LEAROYD'S STORY. (*Soldiers Three.*) — A rich, unprincipled woman bribes Learoyd to capture and deliver to her, when she is about to depart for the season, a neighbor's dog, whom she greatly covets. Mulvaney and Ortheris, on being let into the secret, wish to improve upon the plan and fetch the reward at smaller risk. The "Canteen Sargint's " dog, almost a fac-simile of the other, though as fiendish in temper as "Rip" is angelic, is caught, and his fur painted by Ortheris until he is, to the smallest ring on his tail, a perfect copy. The money is received, and the cur, shut in a basket, is placed in the woman's hands at the railway station. The three conspirators divide the profits of their rascality.

"Nothing short of a masterpiece." — *Athenæum.*

QUIQUERN. (*Second Jungle Book.*) — The story of a famine in an Arctic village during an ice-locked winter, and of the final rescue from starvation brought about through the courage and fortitude of Kotuko, the boy, and the sagacity of two Esquimaux dogs. Kotuko attributed all the credit to his *tornaq*, or guardian spirit.

RECESSIONAL, THE. — A poem written for the Queen's Jubilee and contributed to the London *Times*, July 17, 1897. A page editorial on the "Recessional " in the *Spec-*

tator for July 24, 1897, is entitled, " Mr. Kipling's Hymn."

" In his ' Recessional ' Mr. Kipling has interpreted the feeling of the nation with an insight and a force which are truly marvellous."—*Spectator*.

" Probably Kipling's noblest and most enduring poetic achievement." — *James Lane Allen*.

" It fell upon us as a solemn warning that sobered a whole empire. . . . It raised the ideals of all our people." — *Sir Walter Besant*.

" The beginning of Mr. Kipling's leadership — for he is an Anglo-Saxon leader, say what we may — was the ' Recessional.' People then for the first time recognized that an eloquent advocate of imperialism and national rectitude was continually on the watch. From that time there have been in the public mind two Kiplings — Kipling the great story-teller and Kipling a national stimulus and guide." — *Academy*.

See " Hymn Before Action."

RECORD OF BADALIA HERODSFOOT, THE. (*Many Inventions.*) — Badalia Herodsfoot is a woman of the London slums, deserted by her drunken husband, and enlisted by a devout young curate in the work of distributing relief among her neighbors. She secretly loves the curate, who in turn is in love with Sister Eva, a companion-worker from his own social class. Badalia's husband finally returns, drunk, and demanding money. On the woman's refusal to yield the sum intrusted to her keeping by the clergyman, the man strikes and mortally wounds her. The curate and Eva are summoned to Badalia's death-bed. The dying woman attempts to shield her husband, and, confessing with regard to the curate that she'd " sooner ha' took

up with 'im than any one," counsels him to wed Sister
Eva. Her final injunction is, "Make it a four-pound-ten
funeral — with a pall."

"A little too cynical and brutal to come straight
from life." — *Edmund Gosse.*

"One long exemplification of the gratuitously brutal
method." — *Edinburgh Review.*

"It illustrates Mr. Kipling's remarkable power of
assimilating new details of local color and dialect."—
Athenæum.

"Merely a very clever man's treatment of a land he
knows little of."— *J. M. Barrie,* 1891.

RED DOG. (*Second Jungle Book.*) — A ferocious pack
of dholes or red hunting-dogs, fiercer even than wolves,
have set out, two hundred strong, to kill the jungle people.
Mowgli successfully carries out a plan devised by Kaa.
The enemy is lured to a stream in the banks of which hive
the black wild bees of India, who attack all intruders.
These "Little People of the Rocks" kill several of the
dholes, and as the remainder strive to escape, Mowgli's
knife finishes many, and his companions slay the rest.
This proves to be the last fight of Akela, the "Lone Wolf,"
who sings the death-song and falls dead at Mowgli's feet.

"A story that takes one's breath away. . . .
The narrative is so powerful and original in its manner
that hardly a hint can be given of its strength and quality." — *Joel Chandler Harris.*

REINGELDER AND THE GERMAN FLAG. (*Life's Handicap.*) — The "German Flag" is a small tropical snake,
so named because of its coloring. Breitmann, a German
orchid collector, tells the story of Reingelder, a brother
naturalist, whose hobby was coral-snakes. It was in Ura-

guay that the latter received from a native the gift of a live
" German Flag" in a bottle.   Relying on what he supposed to be good authority, he handled the snake freely,
supposing that its bite was not poisonous.   He was bitten
and died.

> " An admirable piece of grotesque humor. . . .
> It is a delightful study of the stolid egotism of the
> middle-class German *savant*, with his assumption that
> every one is ignorant beside himself." — *Edinburgh
> Review.*

RESCUE OF PLUFFLES, THE.   (*Plain Tales.*) — Pluffles, a callow subaltern of four-and-twenty, was rescued by
Mrs. Hauksbee from the toils of Mrs. Reiver — the lady
" wicked in a business-like way " — and restored to his
English fiancée, whom in his infatuation he had all but
given over.   Mrs. Hauksbee kept the boy under her wing
till "both the ' I wills ' had been said."   After his marriage
Pluffles left the service and went Home.

RETURN OF IMRAY, THE.   (*Life's Handicap.*) — Imray mysteriously disappeared.   His bungalow was after a
time rented by Strickland, of the police.   On overhauling
the ceiling-cloth to remove some troublesome snakes he discovered the corpse of Imray.   The confession was at last
extorted from Bahadur Khan, the native servant, that he
had murdered his former master and had hidden the body.
Threatened with hanging, the man anticipated justice by
allowing one of the snakes, which was half dead, to bite
his naked foot.

RHYME OF THE THREE CAPTAINS, THE.   (*Ballads.*)
— This ballad refers ostensibly to one of the exploits of
Paul Jones, the American pirate.   A trading-brig, hav-

ing sailed " unscathed from a heathen port," is " robbed on a Christian coast," but Jones' privateer succeeds in evading punishment from the ships of the fleet, much to the skipper's disgust.

> For the inner allegorical meaning of " The Rhyme of the Three Captains " see the Harper & Brothers *vs.* Kipling controversy in *Athenæum,* 1890.

RHYME OF THE THREE SEALERS, THE. (*The Seven Seas.*) — The story, in swinging ballad measure, of a bloody fight between the crews of rival poaching-vessels, which meet in a heavy fog on the sealing-grounds, and battle to the death.

> " Magnificent." — *Academy.*

RIKKI–TIKKI–TAVI. (*Jungle Book.*) — Relates how a mongoose, the pet of a small English boy in India, twice saved the lad's life and once the lives of his father and mother. The fights of the mongoose (whose name gives the title to the story) with Karait, the little brown snake, with Nag, the black five-foot cobra, and with Nagaina, the vicious wife of Nag, are described with much humor and spirit.

> " A delicious story." — *Athenæum.*
>
> " Rikki Tikki, though only a mongoose, fights his way gallantly enough into the list of Mr. Kipling's immortals. The history of his war with the cobras is entirely delightful, and refuses to be forgotten." — *Academy.*

RIPPLE SONG, A. — A poem, notable for grace and subtlety, following " The Undertakers " in the *Second Jungle Book.*

ROAD SONG OF THE BANDAR LOG. — An amusing song

supposed to be sung by the Monkey people. It begins, "Here we go in a flung festoon," and its refrain is, "Brother, thy tail hangs down behind." These stanzas follow "Kaa's Hunting" in the *Jungle Book*.

ROSES RED AND ROSES WHITE. — First line of the poem "Blue Roses," which is prefixed to Chapter VII. of *The Light that Failed.*

ROUT OF THE WHITE HUSSARS, THE. (*Plain Tales.*) — The terrified flight of the Hussars was not in the face of the enemy, but in the presence of the regimental drum-horse (who was supposed recently to have died and been buried), dressed like a ghost, and bearing on his back a skeleton. The trick, perpetrated by an Irish subaltern, was played primarily on the colonel, who had cast the beloved drum-horse from the service. The colonel's final decision that since the old horse had proved capable of cutting up the whole regiment he should be returned to his post at the head of the band was received with cheers.

> "It would be hard to find a parallel of its own class to 'The Rout of the White Hussars,' with its study of the effects of what is believed to be supernatural on a gathering of young fellows who are absolutely without fear of any phenomenon of which they comprehend the nature." — *Edmund Gosse.*

ROUTE MARCHIN'. (*Ballads.*) — The song of a regiment

"Marchin' on relief over Injia's sunny plains,
A little front o' Christmas-time an' just be'ind the Rains."

SACRIFICE OF ER-HEB, THE. (*Ballads.*) — A blank-verse narrative setting forth how Bisesa, a beautiful maiden, offered her life as a sacrifice to the angry god Taman in order to save her tribe from "the Sickness." The girl's death appeased Taman, and the epidemic ceased.

SAPPERS. (*The Seven Seas.*) — A defence of their especial work by Her Majesty's Royal Engineers, who modestly believe

"There's only one Corps which is perfect — that's us."

SCREW-GUNS. (*Ballads.*) — The title of this army song explains its theme. It has a very rhythmical movement.

SEA-WIFE, THE. (*The Seven Seas.*) — A ballad of England, the sea-wife, who

"Breeds a breed o' rovin' men
And casts them over sea."

SECOND-RATE WOMAN, A. (*Under the Deodars*).— Mrs. Delville, "The Dowd," was an especial aversion of Mrs. Hauksbee. She dressed shabbily, she walked badly, she dropped her g's. But on one occasion when Mrs. Hauksbee had tried to save a neighbor's sick child and had quite given up hope, the Dowd shuffled in at the opportune moment and rescued the baby's life. The result may be told in Mrs. Hauksbee's words : "So nobody died, and everything went off as it should, and I kissed the Dowd, Polly."

SENDING OF DANA DA, THE. (*In Black and White.*) — Dana Da, an Oriental Yankee, plays upon the credulity of a cult of psychical experimenters in India, and accomplishes an apparent miracle which results in many rupees to himself, not a little mystification to outside observers, and much holy rapture to adherents of the "Tea Cup Creed." He confesses on his death-bed to the simple trick by which he has wrought his manifestations.

SERGEANT'S WEDDIN', THE. (*The Seven Seas.*) — A private tells the story. It is plain that he has no love either for the officer or for his bride.

SESTINA OF THE TRAMP–ROYAL. (*The Seven Seas.*) — One of Kipling's rare experiments in artificial verse-forms. So skilfully is it done that all sense of effort is successfully hidden. The poem contains a very noble and optimistic philosophy of life.

SHILLIN' A DAY. (*Ballads.*) — An old soldier who has fought for the Queen in every part of India and is now "cast from the service" talks of his poverty and tells of his past.

SHIP THAT FOUND HERSELF, THE. (*Day's Work.*) — Mr. Kipling, who is in the confidence of all animate and inanimate things, assures us that it takes a good while for a newly-launched vessel to find herself. Until she does, all the separate pieces chatter among themselves regarding their respective duties ; but the talking finally melts into one voice, which is the conscious soul of the ship. It was so with the cargo-steamer "Dimbula," bound for New York, and this romance of marine mechanism has for principal characters such personages as steam cylinders, deck-beams, and bow-plates.

> A writer in *Macmillan's* (December, 1898) considers this story an allegory — "Servants of the State have to realize that they are parts of a machine, the whole of which depends on the loyalty of every part."

SHIV AND THE GRASSHOPPER. — A three-stanza poem following "Toomai of the Elephants" in the *Jungle Book*. It is a lullaby that Toomai's mother sang to the baby.

SHUT--EYE SENTRY, THE. (*The Seven Seas.*) — A

ballad giving "the story of the implicit or constructive per-jury of thirty sergeants, forty-one corporals, and nine hundred rank and file to save their orderly officer from a charge of drunkenness." The *Academy*, while admitting the great strength of this poem, questions Mr. Kipling's right to treat such a subject. It raises, also, a similar query regarding "That Day."

SLAVES OF THE LAMP. — A tale in two parts, *McClure's Magazine*, August, 1897. The principal personages in Part One are "Stalky" Corkran, or the Slave of the Lamp, Beetle, or Master Gigadibs, and McTurk, or Turkey. Re-enforced by three other young collegians from the "down-stairs study," they are practising for amateur theatricals when their rehearsal is suddenly broken up by King, "the most hated of the house-masters." The rest of the tale is concerned with the laughable and humiliating re-venge which Stalky and Co. took on their priggish in-structor. Part Two introduces us to the same group, who have a reunion after the lapse of fifteen years. Only Stalky is absent, but it is about Stalky that the interest centres. He is as much the hero of the circle as ever, and it is with a story of his plucky exploits in the British army, illustrating his well-known trait of "stalkiness," that the tale concludes.

SMITH ADMINISTRATION. — (See *From Sea to Sea*.)

SNARLEYOW. (*Ballads.*) — A tragic incident of battle from which Tommy draws a lesson :

"The moril of this story, it is plainly to be seen :
You 'aven't got no families when servin' of the Queen —
You 'aven't got no brothers, fathers, sisters, wives, or sons —
If you want to win your battles take an' work your bloomin'
    guns ! "

Soldier an' Sailor Too. (*The Seven Seas.*) — In this rattling song a British soldier describes the marines in the service, who are members neither of any regiment nor of any crew. His opinion of them is a mixture of prejudice, dislike, and admiration.

> " This is a poem springing with spirit ; Mr. Kipling uses its common words as though they were the weapons, the fire, and the crowns of war — and these, indeed, he makes them." — *Academy.*

Soldier, Soldier. (*Ballads.*) — A dialogue between a returned British soldier and an English girl who has lost her lover in the war.

Soldier Tales. — A book of military tales selected from Kipling's works, and published by Macmillan in 1896. It has more than twenty page-illustrations by A. S. Hartrick. The stories are : " With the Main Guard ; " " Drums of the Fore and Aft ; " " Man who Was ; " " Courting of Dinah Shadd ; " " Incarnation of Krishna Mulvaney ; " " Taking of Lungtungpen ; " and " Madness of Private Ortheris."

Solid Muldoon, The. (*Soldiers Three.*) — Mulvaney tells of the day fourteen years before when he " fought wid woman, man, and divil all in the heart av an hour." The woman was Annie Bragin, who " had eyes like the brown av a buttherfly's wing whin the sun catches ut ; " the man was Annie's jealous husband; the devil was incarnate in the ghost of Corporal Flahy, who after his wife's death from cholera " walked afther they buried him, huntin' for her."

Song of Kabir, A. — A poem following " The Miracle of Purun Bhagat " in the *Second Jungle Book.*

SONG OF THE BANJO, THE. (*The Seven Seas.*) — The army banjo, which travels "with the cooking-pots and pails," or "sandwiched 'tween the coffee and the pork," sings of her experiences in all quarters of the world. An amazingly clever, if somewhat artificial, poem.

> "For sheer ingenuity and lightness of touch, 'The Song of the Banjo' cannot be matched." — *Blackwoods*.

SONG OF THE ENGLISH, A. (*The Seven Seas.*) — A group of lyrics, including "The Coastwise Lights," "The Song of the Dead," "The Deep-sea Cables," "The Song of the Sons," "The Song of the Cities," and "England's Answer." Of these, the least successful, perhaps, is "The Song of the Cities," but no one of them is lacking in superb lines.

> "'A Song of the English,' with its ballads and interludes, is the cantata of a master." — *E. C. Stedman*.

SONG OF THE LITTLE HUNTER, THE. — A three-stanza poem, with a very musical movement, following "The King's Ankus" in the *Second Jungle Book*.

SPRING RUNNING, THE. (*Second Jungle Book.*) — Mowgli is now nearly seventeen years old. It is the end of the cold weather, and Spring, "The Time of New Talk," approaches. Mowgli's joy in the season is mingled with a restless unhappiness. His "running" leads him to the village where Messua lives, and he is given cordial welcome. On returning to the Jungle, Mowgli bids farewell to his friends and prepares to take up his home among men. Filled with passages of exquisite description.

STALKY AND Co. — A story of school-boy life published serially in *McClure's Magazine*, Dec., 1898–June, 1899.

The titles of the instalments in their order are as follows :
"Stalky," An Unsavory Interlude ; The Impressionists ;
The Moral Reformers ; A Little Prep. ; The Flag of
their Country ; The Last Term.   The chief characters
are Stalky, McTurk, and Beetle, introduced to the readers
of *McClure's* in *Slaves of the Lamp*, August, 1897.   In
the first chapter, Corkran receives his nickname, Stalky,
by which he is henceforth familiarly known.   " ' Stalky,'
in the school vocabulary, meant clever, well-considered,
and wily, as applied to a plan of action ; and stalkiness was
the one virtue Corkran toiled after."   McTurk is a young
Irishman ; Beetle, who wears glasses and writes poetry, is
Mr. Kipling himself, so we have been informed by Mr.
M. G. White, an old schoolmate ; and the " Coll." is
the well-known Devonshire college of Westward Ho,
where Mr. Kipling received his schooling.

Story of Muhammad Din, The.   (*Plain Tales.*) —
A sympathetic study of child-life.   Little Muhammad Din
becomes friends with the author and builds wonderful pal-
aces in his garden.   One morning the Sahib misses the
boy, and soon learns that he is down with the fever.   A
week later he meets the father of the child carrying in his
arms to the Mussulman burying-ground the tiny body of
Muhammad Din.

"Nowhere in his more elaborate efforts to delineate
child-life . . . does he give us so perfect a piece of
work as the little child-idyl called " The Story of Muhammad Din." — *Francis Adams, Fortnightly*.

" A pathetic masterpiece." — *Edinburgh Review*.

Story of the Gadsbys, The. — I.   " Poor Dear
Mamma."   The scene shifts from the interior of Miss
Minnie Threegan's bedroom at Simla to her mamma's

drawing-room.   Miss Threegan's first meeting with Captain Gadsby is described with much humor.   Poor dear
mamma distinctly loses charm in that officer's eyes as her
daughter gains.   The scene ends with an avowal of the
engagement.

II.   "The World Without."   The engagement of
Captain Gadsby to Miss Minnie Threegan is familiarly discussed in the smoking-room of the Degchi Club by "certain people of importance."   There is plenty of slang,
liquor, and masculine gossip.

III.   "The Tents of Kedar."   Captain Gadsby faces
the uncomfortable duty of breaking the news of his engagement to Mrs. Herriott, a woman deeply in love with him,
with whom he has lived in the most intimate relations.
The scene is a Naini Tal dinner party.   This sketch contains some of Kipling's most telling dialogue.

> "True drawing-room comedy of a high order." —
> *Francis Adams in Fortnightly.*
>
> "The conversation in 'The Tents of Kedar' . . .
> is of consummate adroitness." — *Edmund Gosse.*
>
> For an adverse opinion see *Athenæum*, July 5, 1890.

IV.   "With Any Amazement."   This sketch, taking
its title from the line in the marriage service, "And are
not afraid with any amazement," describes with great
humor Gadsby's wedding-day.   The groom suffers untold
tortures, but the best man, Captain Mafflim, remains loyal
to the last.

V.   "The Garden of Eden."   A honeymoon dialogue
between Captain Gadsby, now three weeks a husband, and
his eighteen-year-old wife.   A specimen :

"Mrs. G.   'D'you know that we're two solemn, serious, grown-up people ?'

"Capt. G. (Tilting her straw hat over her eyes.)
'You grown up! Pooh! You're a baby.'

"Mrs. G. 'And we're talking nonsense.'

"Capt. G. 'Then let's go on talking nonsense.'"

VI. "Fatima." This sketch, the scene of which is
laid in the Gadsbys' bungalow in the Plains, has for its
motto, "And you may go into every room of the house
and see everything that is there, but into the Blue Room
you must *not* go." (*Story of Bluebeard.*) Minnie
Gadsby, not content with the other apartments of her
husband's life, prys into the Blue Room and discovers —
Mrs. Harriet Herriott.

VII. "The Valley of the Shadow." Scene — The
Gadsbys' bungalow in the Plains. Time — 3.40 A. M. of
a hot night about two years after Captain Gadsby's marriage. Mrs. Gadsby is terribly ill and the doctor is fighting for her life. The woman's delirious babble, her husband's broken and frantic words, the Junior Chaplain's
platitudes, and the physician's cool orders, make up a varied
and moving dramatic sketch. Mrs. Gadsby recovers.

> "The pathos of the little bride's delirium in 'The
> Valley of the Shadow' is of a very high, almost of the
> highest, order." — *Gosse.*

VIII. "The Swelling of Jordan." This concluding
scene introduces us to Gadsby Junior (*alias* the Brigadier),
aged ten months. Captain Gadsby seriously considers re-
signing from the service, on the ostensible ground of his
duty to wife and child, and to his family at home. The
story raises the query whether marriage has made a coward
of him. Captain Mafflim has an opinion on the subject.

> "*The Gadsbys* is the most amazing monument of
> precocity in all literature." — *Blackwoods.*

> "The author's cynicism on the subject of Anglo-Indian life comes to a head in the story, cast in dramatic form, of *The Gadsbys*. . . . The whole production is vulgar in style and in tone from beginning to end."
> — *Edinburgh Review*.

STORY OF UNG, THE. (*The Seven Seas*.) — Ung, who made pictures of mammoth and aurochs on bone, learned through bitter disappointments a secret which it were well for modern artists to heed.

STRANGE RIDE OF MORROWBIE JUKES, THE. (*Phantom 'Rickshaw, etc.*) — Jukes, a civil engineer in the Indian service, fell into a hideous Village of Living-Dead. The description of this horseshoe-shaped crater of sand with steeply-graded walls, broad bottom, quicksand entrance, and badger-holes about the sides wherein lived doomed human victims, is Defoe-like in its realism. The frantic attempts to get out of the death-trap, the revolting methods of obtaining food, the treachery of the ex-Brahmin, Gunga Dass, and the final escape of the Englishman, are related with such cool verisimilitude that the absurdity of the plot is successfully concealed.

> "The overwhelming and Poe-like horror of the situation, and the extreme novelty of the conception."
> — *Gosse*.

> "A nightmare more perfect and terrible, I think, than anything of Edgar Poe's." — *Andrew Lang*.

> "One of the most powerful short stories ever written." — *The World, London*.

TAKING OF LUNGTUNGPEN, THE. (*Plain Tales*.) — Mulvaney relates how a detachment of twenty-six men, after swimming a river at night, captured, when "as nakid as Vanus," the native town of Lungtungpen. This was the only occasion on which Mulvaney ever blushed. It increased his faith in the British army, however. "They tuk Lungtungpen nakid ; an' they'd take St. Petersburg in their dhrawers. Begad, they would that !"

> "Those who have not read this little masterpiece have yet before them the pleasure of becoming acquainted with one of the best short stories not merely in English, but in any language." — *Gosse.*

> "There is no funnier episode in the adventures of Don Quixote." — *John D. Adams in Book Buyer,* 1896.

THAT DAY. (*The Seven Seas.*) — A soldier recalls with shame a certain battle which ended in disgraceful panic and flight.

> "I wish I was dead 'fore I done what I did
> Or seen what I seed that day !"[1]

THERE IS PLEASURE IN THE WET, WET CLAY. — First line of the piece of eccentric versification preceding Chapter Seven of *The Naulahka.*

> "For pure poetical prestidigitation we never read anything to compare with the stanza prefixed to Chapter VII. of *The Naulahka.*" — *Blackwoods.*

THREE AND — AN EXTRA. (*Plain Tales.*) — Tells of a woman who mourned so inconsolably at the death of her baby that her husband found her company cheerless, and drifted into gay society where Mrs. Hauksbee (introduced to us in this story and frequently to appear hereafter) annexed him. Several kind lady friends explained the situation at length to the wife, who, waking up to the fact that "the memory of a dead child was worth considerably less

---

[1] See the "Shut-Eye Sentry."

than the affections of a living husband," set herself to the
task of winning back the man's loyalty.   Being clever and
beautiful, as well as good, she succeeded.

THREE-DECKER, THE.   (*The Seven Seas.*) — In answer to the familiar cry of critics, "The three-volume
novel is extinct," Kipling argues the case for romanticism
very cleverly in this parable of the three-decker which carries "Tired people to the Islands of the Blest ! "

THREE MUSKETEERS, THE.   (*Plain Tales.*) — In this
story we have our first introduction to Mulvaney, Learoyd,
and Ortheris.   Mulvaney, assisted by the others, relates
how the three prevented a Thursday regimental parade
coming off, to have been given in honor of an obnoxious
visiting nobleman.   They paid a man to drive with the
unsuspecting lord into a swamp where there was to be an
overturning, a setting-upon by some fellows bribed to per-
sonate thieves, and then a rescue by the three conspirators.
The plot succeeded.   Not only did the nobleman spend
Thursday in the hospital, but the rescuers were liberally
rewarded for gallantry.

THROUGH THE FIRE.   (*Life's Handicap.*) — Athira,
the wife of Madu, a charcoal-burner, runs away with Suket
Singh, and is at first very happy.   But Madu sends after
her the curse of Juseen Dazé, the wizard man, and she begins
to wither away with fear.   Finally she is induced to
return, but her lover will not ler her come alone.   Night
has fallen.   They find the stack of dry wood for the next
day's charcoal-burning on the hill above Madu's house.
On this pyre, after lighting the pile at the four corners,
Suket shoots the woman and then himself.

"'Through the Fire' shows that one Englishman

at least has imagination enough to comprehend the workings of the Oriental mind." — *Critic.*

THROWN AWAY. (*Plain Tales.*) — The story of a boy who was reared by his parents in England under the "sheltered life system," and who, on reaching India and getting away from their surveillance, reacted from his training, and ended a career of dissipation in suicide. His comrades, wishing to spare the feelings of his family at home, concocted a story of the boy's death from cholera.

> "The very remarkable story of 'Thrown Away' is as hopelessly tragic as any in Mr. Kipling's somewhat grim repertory." — *Gosse.*

"TIGER! TIGER!" (*Jungle Book.*) — Mowgli, cast out from the wolf-pack, escaped to a village inhabited by Man. He was approached with wonder and distrust, but finally found a home with Messua, wife of the richest villager. While acting as village herd, he killed Shere Khan, his old enemy, but this failed to add to his doubtful popularity. Accused of sorcery, the lad was driven away, and he returned to the forest. "Man Pack and Wolf Pack have cast me out," said Mowgli. "Now I will hunt alone in the jungle."

TO BE FILED FOR REFERENCE. (*Plain Tales.*) — McIntosh Jellaludin is a former Oxford man who has turned Mohammedan, married a native woman, and nearly ruined a remarkable mind by habitual drunkenness. On his deathbed he bequeathes to the author the MS. of a book which he assures him will make him famous. "It is a great work," he says, "and I have paid for it in seven years' damnation."

TO THE TRUE ROMANCE. (*The Seven Seas.*) — This lyric, originally the prefatory poem in *Many Inven-*

tions and now included in *The Seven Seas,* is a reverent tribute to the "True Romance," which is

> "In sooth that lovely Truth
> The careless angels know !"

> "One of Kipling's most beautiful poems, and one in which he gives expression to his deepest self. . . . It is this poem which, more than any other, gives the key to the interpretation of Mr. Kipling's work in general, and displays its controlling aim." — *Charles Eliot Norton in Atlantic.*

Tods' Amendment. (*Plain Tales.*) — Tods, a precocious English six-year-old, mingles much with the natives and speaks the vernacular. He is present at a dinner-party of his mamma's where one of the guests is the "Legal Member," who has helped frame a highly obnoxious Land Bill. The talk drifts to the subject of land-tenure, and the child, to the surprise of the company, joins in the conversation and repeats some remarks, uncomplimentary to the framers of the Bill, made by his humble friends. The great man is so influenced by this new light thrown on his measure that he introduces into the Bill "Tods' Amendment."

> "'Tods' Amendment' is in itself a political allegory. . . . What led to the story, one sees without difficulty, was the wish to emphasize the fact that unless the Indian Government humbles itself and becomes like Tods, it can never legislate with efficiency, because it never can tell what all the *jhampanies* and *saises* in the bazar really wish for." — *Gosse.*

Tomb of His Ancestors, The. (*Day's Work.*) — A young British officer who inherits many striking characteristics of his dead grandfather is received on arriving in

India with superstitious reverence by the Bhils, a wild native tribe. They believe that the departed Sahib, who "had made them men" and whom they regard as their tutelary deity, is now reincarnated. The tribe weave supernatural legends about the young man and obey his slightest word as if it were that of a god. At his command they restore stolen property and even submit to the hated ordeal of vaccination.

"The best of the present volume [D. W.], in our judgment, is 'The Tomb of His Ancestors.'" — *Literature*.

TOMLINSON. (*Ballads*.) — A poem of grotesque and terrible power which well illustrates Kipling's strenuous philosophy of life. Tomlinson was a characterless, lukewarm creature, who, from lack of positive virtues, was refused admission to Heaven and from weakness and lack of wilful sin was scornfully rejected by Hell also.

"There are powerful passages here and there in the poem, but as a whole it is what we call splatter-dash writing." — *Edinburgh Review*.

"A gruesome satire on the lukewarm sin, the limp selfishness of modern days." — *Spectator*.

"The delightful satire of 'Tomlinson.'" — *Academy*.

TOMMY. (*Ballads*.) — One of the most widely known and liked of the *Ballads*. Tommy Atkins contrasts the way in which he is ordinarily treated and spoken to by the English civilian with the conduct and speech he receives when "there's trouble in the wind."

TOOMAI OF THE ELEPHANTS. (*Jungle Book*.) — Little Toomai, ten-year-old son of an elephant driver, was rebuked by "Peterson Sahib" for recklessly stepping among the beasts at a Keddah stockade. "Must I never go there?" the boy asked. "Yes," was the answer. "When thou hast seen the elephants dance." The child took this proverbial expression, which is equivalent to "never," seriously. His wish was unexpectedly answered. He was keeping guard over his elephant one night when the latter broke away and headed toward the forest. Toomai was soon upon his back, and presently found himself in one of those rare gatherings of wild elephants in the heart of the Garo hills. They stamped together in noisy rhythm, as if dancing. On his safe return, Little Toomai was received with great honor, and was straightway christened "Toomai of the Elephants."

"Best of all, in imaginative scope and descriptive power, we hold to be 'Toomai of the Elephants.' The account of the night journey of Kala Nag and his tiny rider to the 'Tanz-Platz' of these mysterious quadrupeds is simply stupendous." — *Athenæum.*

TRACK OF A LIE, THE. (*Phantom 'Rickshaw.*) Illustrates the train of consequences that may follow even the utterance of a jest. The idle remark of a club-man was turned by a journalist into a newspaper paragraph, which made the circle of the globe.

TROOPIN'. (*Ballads.*) — A British soldier, whose time has just expired, is jubilant over the prospect of returning home.

"We're goin' 'ome, we're goin' 'ome,
    Our ship is *at* the shore,
An' you must pack your 'aversack,
    For we won't come back no more."

TRUCE OF THE BEAR, THE. — A very forcible ballad,

published in *Literature*, Oct. 1, 1898. The poem is, on the surface, a spirited account of a bear hunt ; it can hardly be doubted, however, that its purpose is allegorical. Its appearance shortly after the Czar's proclamation in behalf of universal disarmament lends color to the belief that the burden of the poem, " Make ye no truce with Adam-zad — the bear that walks like a man," expresses distrust of that monarch's motive. The New York *Nation*, which shares this general view, has dubbed the ballad "Kipling's Retrocessional."

UNDERTAKERS THE. (*Second Jungle Book.*) — During a conversation between a Mugger, an Adjutant-crane, and a jackal, the Mugger (crocodile) relates how once he had risen to the river's surface and striven unsuccessfully to seize the hands of a child which were trailed over the side of a boat. After telling his tale, the beast goes off to doze on a sand-bar. Here he is presently discovered and shot dead by a passing Englishman. " The last time that I had my hand in a Mugger's mouth," the man says, stooping over the huge jaws, — and then he tells the story already related. He is the child grown to manhood.

> "One of the finest chapters of all in the *Jungle Book.*" — *Edinburgh Review*.

VAMPIRE, THE. — A poem written to accompany a picture by Philip Burne-Jones in the New Gallery. The lines were printed in the London *Daily Mail* in April, 1897. They were quoted in the *Critic* for May 8, 1897, and have been frequently republished since. The first stanza is as follows :

" A fool there was and he made his prayer
    (Even as you and I !)
To a rag and a bone and a hank of hair
(We called her the woman who did not care),
But the fool he called her his lady fair
    (Even as you and I !) "

> " A tremendously powerful and strikingly original and realistic variation of the eternal plaint against woman." — *Editorial in Boston Transcript.*
>
> " The metrical manner of ' The Vampire ' is that of Poe in his ballad of ' Annabel Lee.' " — *Henry Austin in Dial.*

VENUS ANNODOMINI. (*Plain Tales.*) — Gayerson, very young and impressionable, thought himself deeply in love with a handsome, middle-aged beauty who looked half her age. His recovery was brought about in part by the advent of his father, who revealed the fact that he had himself worshipped the woman in his youth. He was cured perhaps quite as much by meeting her nineteen-year-old daughter.

WALKING DELEGATE, A. (*Day's Work.*) — A yellow horse from Kansas tries to spread sedition among a company of equine acquaintances in a Vermont pasture, but his doctrine that all horses are free and equal and that they should rise against their oppressor, Man, meets with very forcible opposition. Despite some touches of humor and much clever dialect this story must be reckoned as among Mr. Kipling's least successful ventures.

> " ' A Walking Delegate ' is an allegory naked and not ashamed. Mr. Kipling has a profound antipathy to Socialism, and a profound belief in 'the day's work.' . . . But he has now chosen to represent the contempt

of real workers for the idle demagogue in terms of horseflesh, and the result is, to speak plainly, nonsense." — *Macmillan's Magazine.*

WANDERING JEW, THE. (*Life's Handicap.*) — John Hay was rich but unhappy, for he feared to die. On learning that in going once round the world in an easterly direction he could gain one day, he made the trip, and delighted with its success, continued for years circling the earth with his face to the rising sun. A doctor, put on the track of the man, caught him in Madras and persuaded him that he could gain immortality much more easily through sitting in a chair suspended by ropes from the roof of a room and letting the earth swing free under him. Thus he would gain a day in a day and be the equal of the undying sun. The counsel was followed, and there to-day, a stop-watch in his hand, racing against eternity, sits John Hay, the immortal.

"Such tawdry trifles as 'The Lang Men o' Larut' or 'The Wandering Jew.'" — *Athenæum.*

WATCHES OF THE NIGHT. (*Plain Tales.*) — This story is a comment on the fact that "many religious people are deeply suspicious." A colonel's wife was led by circumstantial evidence and the promptings of her temperament to suspect her excellent husband of infidelity to the marriage bond. She accused him of his crime with language scriptural and to the point. Thenceforth they lived together in wretched estrangement. The whole tragedy might have been averted if the wife had possessed the explanation of the suspicious circumstances which is given in the story.

WAYSIDE COMEDY, A. (*Under the Deodars.*) — This powerful but unpleasant story of marital jealousy and hatred is framed in the setting of a lonely station in the Hills which contains five English people — the *dramatis personæ* of the tale. These are, Major Vansuythen, virtuous but stupid ; his wife, whose only fault is that she is beautiful ; Mrs. Boulte, in her heart unfaithful to her husband, and in love with Ted Kurrell ; Kurrell, a scoundrel who has transferred his affections from Mrs. Boulte to Mrs. Vansuythen; and Boulte, tired of his wife, and enslaved to the common charmer, who repulses both him and Kurrell. The state of things becomes known to each of the five, except the Major. The four come to hate and despise each other, but the good Major wonders why they are not more social.

WEE WILLIE WINKIE. (*Wee Willie Winkie, and Other Stories.*) — Wee Willie Winkie, the freckled six-year-old, by rescuing a young lady from a dangerous predicament and probably saving her life, enters into his manhood and becomes thenceforth Percival William Williams. The precocious behavior attributed to the little son of the Colonel fails to be convincing. Indeed, this tale, while worth reading for the sake of several charming episodes and bits of dialogue, is the most unnatural of Kipling's child-stories.

"To criticise the story, which is told with infinite zest and picturesqueness, seems merely priggish. Yet if Wee Willie Winkie had been twelve instead of six, the feat would have been just possible. . . . In all this Mr. Kipling, led away by sentiment and a false ideal, is not quite the honest craftsman that he should be." — *Gosse.*

WHEN 'OMER SMOTE 'IS BLOOMIN' LYRE. (*The Seven Seas.*) — The first line of a witty lyric preceding the

" Barrack-room Ballads " in *The Seven Seas*.   It is a very original disclaimer of originality.

WHITE HORSES. — A lyric of eighty lines (ten double quatrains) which appeared in *Literature*, Vol. I., No. 1, October 23, 1897.   It begins :

> " Where run your colts at pasture ?
> Where hide your mares to breed ? "

Professor Barrett Wendell, writing in the New York *Times*, has words of praise for this imaginative poem, but complains of its obscurity.[1]

> The " White Horses " apparently refer to nothing
> more than white-capped ocean waves.

WHITE MAN'S BURDEN, THE. — A poem of seven stanzas, beginning :

> " Take up the White Man's Burden,
> Send forth the best ye breed."

It appeared in *McClure's* for February, 1899.   It has probably been more widely read, discussed, and parodied than any other poem of the time.   Commenting on " The White Man's Burden," Mr. W. T. Stead, in the English *Review of Reviews,* says :   " It is an international document of the first order of importance.   It is a direct appeal to the United States to take up the policy of expansion.   It puts the matter on the highest and most unselfish grounds.   The poet has idealized and transfigured imperialism.   He has shown its essence to be not lordship, but service."

> " That jingo jingle, ' The White Man's Burden.' "
> — *Henry Austin in Dial.*

WHITE SEAL, THE.   (*Jungle Book.*) — Kotick, the

---

[1] See *Literary Digest*, Jan. 1, 1898.

white seal, was so horrified by the sight of men butchering his brother seals at the killing-grounds that he devoted himself to discovering some sheltered beach where men had never come and to guiding the herds thither.   He at last succeeded, but not until he had gone through many dangerous adventures.

> " ' The White Seal ' attracted a good deal of attention when it first appeared, in view of the Behring Sea arbitration, now happily concluded." — *Athenæum.*

WIDOW AT WINDSOR, THE.   (*Ballads.*) — One of " Missis Victorier's sons " sings a song in her praise.   It begins :

> " Ave you 'eard o' the ' Widow at Windsor "
> With a hairy gold crown on 'er 'ead ?
> She 'as ships on the foam — she 'as millions at 'ome,
> An' she pays us poor beggars in red."

WIDOW'S PARTY, THE.   (*Ballads.*) — A soldier relates some of the fortunes of war in the service of Victoria.

> " You can't refuse when you get the card,
> And the Widow gives the party."

WILL YOU NEVER LET US GO ?   Refrain of the striking song of the galley-slave, written by Charlie Mears.[1]

WILLIAM THE CONQUEROR.   (*Day's Work.*) — A tale of the great Famine of the Eight Districts in Southern India.   William the Conqueror is the nickname of Miss Martyn, the heroine, who refuses to leave her brother when he is ordered south for famine duty.   She falls in love with Scott, Martyn's intimate friend and co-laborer in relief distribution.   She likes " men who do things," and Scott is

---

[1] (*See* "The Finest Story in the World.")

one of her kind — a robust type of Englishman who can do the work of five men without making any fuss. When the Madras famine is stamped out and the exiles return to the north for Christmas week, the two are engaged to be married.

> " Gives us a masterly impression of the recent famine and of the efforts made to cope with it." — *L. Zangwill, Cosmopolitan,* 1899.
>
> "One of the finest things Mr. Kipling has ever done." — *McClure's (editorial).*
>
> " If ever there was a story to tell to boys, this ' William the Conqueror ' is that story. It is the real Kipling, with a new note, — the note of pity and kindliness, — a sign of his growth." — *Academy.*

WITH SCINDIA TO DELHI. (*Ballads.*) — An Indian Prince rode fifty miles after a heavy defeat near Delhi, carrying on his saddle-bow a faithful beggar-girl who loved him. He lost her when almost within sight of safety.

WITH THE MAIN GUARD. (*Soldiers Three.*) Mulvaney relieves the heat of a sleepless June night by recounting an exciting battle with a body of "bloomin' Paythans" fought in a "gut betune two hills, as black as a bucket, an' as thin as a girl's waist." The hand-to-hand struggle with knife and bayonet is described with tremendous realism and power. The fury of the Irish troops after the first of their comrades have been slain sweeps everything before it, and justifies Mulvaney's boast : "An Oirish rig'mint is the divil an' more."

> " The battle in the ' Main Guard ' is like Homer or Sir Walter." — *Blackwoods.*

WITHOUT BENEFIT OF CLERGY. (*Life's Handicap.*) — John Holden, an Englishman, bought a Mussulman's daughter from her grasping hag of a mother, and hired a house for the two. Ameera was very beautiful, and passionately adored Holden, who returned her worship. When she bore him a son, Ameera's cup of happiness was full.   But Tota, the "gold-colored little god," after having grown old enough to talk, died of the seasonal autumn fever.   Ameera was completely heart-broken, and Holden hardly less so.   It needed only the death of Ameera herself, which followed not long afterward, from black cholera, to make the man's desolation complete.

> "The tremulous passion of Ameera, her hopes, her fears, and her agonies of disappointment, combine to form by far the most tender page which Mr. Kipling has written." — *Edmund Gosse, Century,* 1891.

WRECK OF THE VISIGOTH, THE. (*Soldiers Three.*) — A steamer-captain tells about the sinking of a five-hundred-ton coasting-trade steamer one hundred miles from land.   The cowardly selfishness of some passengers is contrasted with the bravery of others — notably that of one woman who was among the rescued.

WRESSLEY OF THE FOREIGN OFFICE. (*Plain Tales.*) — Wressley fell in love with a pretty, frivolous girl, and decided that the best work of his career should be laid reverently at her feet.   Hence he wrote an exhaustive history of *Native Rule in Central India,* and after months of toil brought the first copy of his book to Miss Venner.   This is her review : "Oh, your book ? It's all about those howwid Wajahs. I didn't understand it."   The man departed, and destroyed the whole edition of the best book of Indian history ever written.

YOKED WITH AN UNBELIEVER. (*Plain Tales.*) — Phil Garron on sailing for India leaves a sweetheart behind who loves him passionately ; he hopes to work hard and return to marry her. But soon her image begins to fade from Phil's mind. She, on her part, is forced by her parents into an uncongenial marriage. The girl (who still loves him) writes a wild letter, which he, conceiving himself to be mightily slighted, replies to reproachfully. Phil prospers, marries a Hill girl, and settles down happily, though Agnes is thinking of him with undeserved pity. Finally her husband's death releases the woman, and she goes joyfully to seek Phil on his tea plantation. She finds him. He and his wife are very nice to her.

YOUNG BRITISH SOLDIER, THE. (*Ballads.*) — A song of advice composed for the benefit of the "'arf-made recruity." It contains much excellent counsel, and has a roaring chorus.

.007 (*Day's Work.*) — The story of a railway locomotive, relating its introduction to brother engines in the round-house, its forty-mile run with a wrecking-crew to the scene of an accident, and its subsequent election to the Amalgamated Brotherhood of Locomotives. The conversation of the various engines comes as near being convincing as any such essentially artificial dialogue can. The story succeeds in what it attempts, but opinions may differ as to whether the attempt is worth while.

> ".007 is beyond me. Here all Mr. Kipling's manias break loose at once — there is the madness of American slang, the madness of technical jargon, and the madness of believing that silly talk, chiefly consisting of moral truisms, is amusing because you put it into the mouths of machines." — *Macmillan's Magazine.*

> "Unless the reader is an engine-fitter he will not find much pleasure in this bewildering maze of technical terms." — *London Daily Chronicle.*

APPENDIX

CERTAIN SELECTED OPINIONS ON MR. KIPLING'S WORK IN GENERAL

"Burnt into Mr. Kipling's spirit is a touch of that Puritanism which has inspired our empire-builders so largely. . . . Whatever the form, Mr. Kipling is always at bottom in deep and serious earnest. Though so wonderful a master of style and metre and of every form of rhetorical artifice, he never writes for the sake of word-spinning, but always because he has got a nail which he is most anxious to drive in up to the head. . . . Mr. Kipling is, of course, a poet who has always been intensely national in sentiment, but he is also a great master of literary technique, — a conscious artist in words who has laid himself out to study language as men study a science, and to wring from it all its secrets and all its latent possibilities. We know what happens in France when men do that — how the artist eats up the man, and how the inhuman maxim of art for art's sake takes him captive. Imagine the most modern and most artful of the younger French poets being moved to write in the mood of a Hebrew prophet. The thing is inconceivable. He might, no doubt, have produced a great patriotic ode full of fire and splendor; but could he have touched that note of

seriousness which we see in Mr. Kipling's verse ? '' —
Spectator, July 24, 1897 (Editorial).

"Of the many remarkable qualities in Mr. Kipling's
publications, the most remarkable of all is the extraordinary
faculty of observation which they display. . . . Nothing
he comes in contact with seems to escape his notice, and,
while still a young man, he gives one the impression in his
books of having lived two or three lives, and lived them
pretty thoroughly. . . . But of all Mr. Kipling's
works *The Jungle Book*, in two series, is the most remarkable and original, and the one which, so far, offers the best
promise of retaining a permanent place in our literature.
. . . It may be questioned whether compositions
dealing so largely in slang and colloquialisms [*i.e.*, as many
of the stories and ballads do] can ever hope to take a permanent place in literature, however dramatically expressive
they may be for the immediate purpose. . . . Apart
from the question of slang, such sketches of the superficial
manners and talk of the society of the day as are put before
us in *Plain Tales from the Hills*, however clever and
brilliant, form only amusing reading for contemporaries ;
they have no lasting interest. . . . Every now and
then the author has risen above this level, and has shown
that he has it in him to deal with the pathos and the
humor of life in a broader spirit and from a higher point
of view ; but his excursions into these higher regions are
few and transitory. . . . He has to a great extent
been frittering away his remarkable and exceptional powers
in playing to the gallery." — *Edinburgh Review*, 1898.

"The nameless red-haired girl in *The Light that Failed*,
whom for convenience' sake we shall call Anonyma, re-

marks to Dick Heldar, ' Your things smell of tobacco and blood ; can't you do anything but soldiers ? ' Yes, Anonyma, he can do many other things, but the scent which you dislike will hang over them all ; for the ' fog of fighting ' has got into his eyes, and he carries the battle-field wherever he wanders. . . . Vitality at all costs is Mr. Kipling's aim — to be alive and to show it. . . . Mild clear lights are not at all to his liking. Still life is the one kind of life which he would never choose to paint. . . . Vitality, with Mr. Kipling, keeps at a safe distance from refinement. It cannot trust itself in the society of good women or of courteous and self-respecting men. It is loud-voiced and masterful, swaggering about with its hat on one side and its hand perpetually on the hilt of its sword, challenging admiration, and talking, with a boastful air, of horses and ' heterodox women.' . . . If Realism be a volcanic shower of mud and red-hot cinders, burning up the soil on which it falls, then three-fourths of Mr. Kipling's stories are realistic. The fire in them is unmistakable ; but the fountains of mud are blown into the air along with it, and harden on the ground into dead lava." — *Quarterly*, 1892.

" His whole utterance vibrates with an audible, if some-what coarse pulse of feeling, is quickened by a bold, if some-what bravado passion, is instinct with a buccaneer's daring, an imperialist's idealism, a man's fibre and flesh and blood. And it is resonant with corresponding lilt and rhythm. It swings effects on the reader by its flashing, dashing refrains. Neither sensation nor cadence are ever sustained, and both are seldom delicate. They are earthly, but not earthy ; compact of the world, but not of clay. . . . His

men fight and win ; his women love and are lost ; he de-
lights in the fiery, furious moods of humanity and nature ;
he 'rejoices like a giant to run his course ; ' so far there is
something of Byron about him ; in fine, he sings (sometimes whistles) of adventure, like an adventurer.   And yet
he is not destitute of softer intervals, deeper insight, and
sublimer flights. . . . His whole message is informed
with a scorn of the petty and sordid, the sickly and the
maudlin. . . . His enormous directness of animal
vigor, his absolute sincerity and magic insight, above all,
his impetuous audacity. . . . He is truly and powerfully himself.'' — *Quarterly*, 1897.

   ''A glowing imagination, an inexhaustible invention, a
profound knowledge of the human heart — these are three
of his choicest possessions.   Yet how inadequately does so
bald a statement sum up the rich profusion of his talents !
How beggarly and feeble seem the resources of language to
do justice to his great achievements ! '' — *Blackwoods*,
1898.

   ''While Mr. Kipling surveys mankind from China to
Peru, he does so not from the dubious point of view of the
cosmopolitan, but from the firm vantage-ground of a
Briton.'' — *Ibid*.

   '' In the present volume (*Seven Seas*) the cynical reader
will turn to a little group of literary allegories with peculiar
pleasure. 'The Last Rhyme of True Thomas,' 'In the Neolithic Age,' 'The Story of Ung,' 'The Three-Decker'
— all excessively clever, and all written to instruct the reviewer what he is to say, to tell him what his attitude must be.
He is to insure the creator, the manly maker of music, who
' sings of all we fought and feared and felt,' against ' criti-

cism,' by which Mr. Kipling invariably means malignant and envious attack. The public likes this defiant attitude, and the great majority of reviewers are abashed by it." — *Saturday Review.*

" Not since Adam was driven from the Jungle has there been any one to let us in. . . . It has remained for Mr. Kipling to prove to us, above all the warfare of life, the essential brutish brotherhood that links forever all the mouths and stomachs of the world. Basing his work upon the latent Mowgli in us all, he has created one of the most masterful illusions of literature. It almost makes a man think with his stomach to read the *Jungle* through." — *Critic,* Nov. 23, 1895.

" We take Mr. Kipling very seriously, for he is the greatest creative mind that we now have ; he has the de-vouring eye and the portraying hand." — *Atlantic Monthly.*

" Mr. Kipling's work is the art form of Calvinism. When Calvinism was new and fresh in the world, each man was so troubled about the salvation or damnation of his own individual soul, it would seem, that he had no heart or time to work the awful theology over into art. But now that the devil has loosed his hold a bit, and we sit up and look about us in a blinking world, something of the old Greek spirit comes creeping back ; and there arises among us a poet to sing : 'What is to be will be, and it's all in the day's work : let no man, therefore, shirk ; neither let him be afraid.' . . . The law is his master-word — the law of the jungle, the law of the army, the law of Her Majesty's realm, and the law of gravity. Of 'the spirit that giveth life' he has no word to speak." — *J. B. P., in Critic,* November, 1898.

" The secret of his strength lies in the fact that he expresses the force of the deeper-lying human instincts as they are stimulated by the demands of modern life. He bids us listen to them as guiding voices which tell of the long experience of our human ancestors, and of that line of living forms from which the first of human beings was descended. He warns us that these instincts must not be quenched by the artificiality of what we in our pride call our modern civilization ; that they must be modified to harmonize with the complex environment of these later times, rather than bridled into subjection by a confident rationalism which forgets the failures of reason in the past." — *H. R. Marshall in Century.*

" Not infrequent in Mr. Kipling's works is an epic quality, both of imagery and diction, it were vain to seek elsewhere in modern fiction. By such vigorous and vital phrases as ' the dark, stale blood that makes men afraid,' or ' the earth turned to iron lest men should escape by hiding in her,' he produces a direct, irresistible effect. In his love of homely similes, he keeps close to the practice of the great masters of the epic." — *The National Observer.*

" In the wonderful series of lyrics, which have, one after another, within the past five years captured the whole world and become familiar almost to weariness, the great achievement was that in them he restored poetry to the use of the modern world as a real force. In his hands it has ceased to be a plaything of dilettante scholars and artists, and become a mighty and practical instrument, — a weapon of finest temper for polemic controversy, a moral force compared with which the teaching of philosophy, press, and pulpit sounds feeble. It is undoubtedly his very rudeness of strength, use of slang expressions, and coarse realism of which we have spoken, that give his verse such virility and pungency and timeliness, that it can shy its castor into the roped arena of every-day men's combats and excitements, where the æsthetic elegance and high-minded aloofness of Tennyson would be as pathetically ludicrous as a knight stalking about in clanking armor." — *Boston Transcript*, 1899 (Editorial).

BIBLIOGRAPHY OF FIRST EDITIONS

1. SCHOOLBOY LYRICS. Lahore, 1881. *The Civil and Military Gazette.* 16mo, pp. 46.

2. ECHOES. By two writers. Lahore : the *Civil and Military Gazette Press*, 1884. 8vo. (Privately circulated while Kipling was a young man on the staff of *The Civil and Military Gazette.*)

3. QUARTETTE, THE CHRISTMAS ANNUAL OF THE CIVIL AND MILITARY GAZETTE. By Four Anglo-Indian Writers. Lahore, 1885. Gray paper wrapper. 8vo. pp. 125. (Written entirely by members of the Kipling family. Includes "The Phantom 'Rickshaw" and "The Strange Ride of Marrowbie Jukes, C.B.")

4. ON HER MAJESTY'S SERVICE ONLY, DEPARTMENTAL DITTIES, AND OTHER VERSES. To all Heads of Departments and All Anglo-Indians. Rudyard Kipling, Assistant. Department of Public Journalism, Lahore District. 1886. Oblong 8vo. Printed on one side only, on brown paper like a public document, at Lahore, by *The Civil and Military Gazette Press.*

5. DEPARTMENTAL DITTIES. Second edition. Lahore, n. d. (1887 ?). 8vo.
"Second edition of 'Departmental Ditties' had extra verses ; so, I believe, had third." — *Rudyard Kipling.*

6. DEPARTMENTAL DITTIES. Third edition. Lahore (1888 ?). 8vo.

7. PLAIN TALES FROM THE HILLS. Calcutta : Thacker, Spink, & Co. London : W. Thacker & Co. 1888. 12mo. pp. xii–283. Twenty-eight of the forty tales appeared originally in *The Civil and Military Gazette ;* the others were new.

8. SOLDIERS THREE. A Collection of Stories setting forth Certain Passages in the Lives and Adventures of Privates Terence Mulvaney, Stanley Ortheris, and John Learoyd. Done into type and Edited by Rudyard Kipling. Allahabad : Printed at the *Pioneer Press*. 1888. Gray paper covers. 8vo. pp. 97. Issued as No. 1 of A. H. Wheeler & Co.'s Indian Railway Library.

9. THE STORY OF THE GADSBYS. A tale without a plot. Allahabad : A. H. Wheeler & Co. 1888. Gray paper covers. 8vo. pp. vi–100. No. 2 of A. H. Wheeler & Co.'s Indian Railway Library.

10. IN BLACK AND WHITE. Allahabad : A. H. Wheeler & Co. 1888. Gray paper wrappers. 8vo. Introduction. pp. 106. No. 3 of Wheeler's Indian Railway Library.

11. UNDER THE DEODARS. Allahabad : A. H. Wheeler & Co. 1888. Gray paper wrappers. 8vo. Preface. pp. 106. No. 4 of Wheeler's Indian Railway Library.

12. THE PHANTOM 'RICKSHAW, AND OTHER TALES. Allahabad : A. H. Wheeler & Co. 1888. Gray paper wrappers. 8vo. pp. 104. No. 5 of Wheeler's Indian Railway Library.

13. THE PHANTOM 'RICKSHAW, AND OTHER EERIE TALES. First English Edition. 8vo. Original wrappers. London. 1888.

14. WEE WILLIE WINKIE, AND OTHER CHILD STORIES. Allahabad : A. H. Wheeler & Co. 1888. Gray paper covers. 8vo. pp. 96. No. 6 of Wheeler's Indian Railway Library.

15. THE COURTING OF DINAH SHADD, AND OTHER STORIES. With a Biographical and Critical Sketch by Andrew Lang. New York : Harper & Brothers. 1890. Paper covers. Portrait. 12mo. pp. xii–182.

16. DEPARTMENTAL DITTIES, AND OTHER VERSES. Fourth edition. (Containing nine poems not previously collected.) Calcutta. Square 8vo. 1890.

17. THE CITY OF DREADFUL NIGHT, AND OTHER SKETCHES. (Suppressed.) Allahabad. 1890. 8vo. "Of this book an edition of 3,000 copies, printed for Wheeler & Co., was cancelled. Of the edition three copies only were preserved." — Manuscript note on fly-leaf of copy sold in London last December for £22.

18. SOLDIERS THREE, AND OTHER STORIES. First American Edition. 12mo. Original wrappers. New York : John W. Lovell Co. 1890. Prefixed to this edition is a facsimile letter of the author, not published elsewhere.

19. DEPARTMENTAL DITTIES, AND OTHER VERSES. Fifth edition (containing several additional poems). Calcutta : Thacker, Spink & Co. London : W. Thacker & Co. Bombay : Thacker & Co., Limited. 1891. Cloth. 8vo. pp. vi–121.

20. THE CITY OF DREADFUL NIGHT, AND OTHER PLACES. Depicted by Rudyard Kipling. Allahabad : A. H. Wheeler & Co. 1891. Gray paper covers. 8vo. pp. 96. No. 14 of Wheeler's Indian Railway Library. ("Suppressed by me." — Rudyard Kipling.)

21. DEPARTMENTAL DITTIES, AND OTHER VERSES. Sixth edition. 1891. Identical with 5th except for the addition of a glossary of four pages.

22. THE SMITH ADMINISTRATION. (Suppressed.) Allahabad : A. H. Wheeler & Co. 1891. 8vo. "Of this work an edition of 3,000 copies was printed, but owing to a difference of opinion between Rudyard Kipling and the proprietors of the *Pioneer* and *Civil and Military Gazette*, the entire edition was destroyed, with the exception of three copies." — Manuscript note on fly-leaf of one of the three copies sold in London, December, 1898, for £26.

23. THE CITY OF THE DREADFUL NIGHT. First English edition. Allahabad and London. 1891. 8vo. (Should have a slip of apology preceding title.)
24. LIFE'S HANDICAP, BEING STORIES OF MINE OWN PEOPLE. London and New York: Macmillan & Co. 1891. 12mo. pp. xiii–351.
25. THE LIGHT THAT FAILED. Portrait. Philadelphia: J. B. Lippincott Co. (In *Lippincott's Magazine*, January, 1891.) Paper. 8vo. pp. 97. (The text of the first English edition, London, 1891, is very different.)
26. LETTERS OF MARQUE. Allahabad. 1891. A. H. Wheeler & Co. 8vo. pp. iv–154. (Suppressed by author and publisher almost immediately after publication.)
27. WEE WILLIE WINKEE, AND OTHER STORIES. Allahabad and London. 1891. 8vo.
28. AMERICAN NOTES. New York: M. J. Ivers & Co. 1891. Paper. 12mo. pp. 160. (Containing also "The Bottle Imp," by R. L. Stevenson.)
29. MINE OWN PEOPLE. New York: Lovell, Coryell & Company. 1891. With a Critical Introduction by Henry James, and Facsimile of Manuscript Letter by Mr. Kipling. 12mo. pp. xxvi–268.
30. BARRACK-ROOM BALLADS, AND OTHER VERSES. London: Methuen & Co. 1892. 12mo. pp. xix–208. Thirty copies on Japan paper and 225 on large.
31. THE NAULAHKA: A STORY OF WEST AND EAST. London: William Heinemann. 1892. 12mo. pp. vi–276. (An edition with rhymed chapter headings was copyrighted in the same year by Macmillan & Co. "The Naulahka" was written in collaboration with Wolcott Balestier.

32. BALLADS AND BARRACK-ROOM BALLADS.   New York :
    Macmillan & Co., and London.   1892.   12mo.
    pp. xvi–207.

33. DETROIT FREE PRESS CHRISTMAS NUMBER.   Price
    6d.   The Record of Badalia Herodsfoot.   By Rud-
    yard Kipling.   One Day's Courtship.   By Luke Sharp.
    London.   1893.   *Detroit Free Press.*   (Kipling's
    story was published later in " Many Inventions."

34. MANY INVENTIONS.   London : Macmillan & Co., and
    New York, 1893.   12mo.   pp. ix–365.

35. BALLADS AND BARRACK-ROOM BALLADS.   (Contain-
    ing additional poems.)   New York : Macmillan & Co.,
    and London.   1893.   12mo.   pp. xvi–217.

36. MY FIRST BOOK.   The experiences of various con-
    temporary authors.   London : 1894, Chatto & Windus.
    8vo.   (With an article by Kipling.)

37. THE JUNGLE BOOK.   Illustrated by J. L. Kipling, W.
    H. Drake, and P. Frenzeny.   London : Macmillan &
    Co., and New York.   1894.   12mo.   pp. vi–212.

38. THE SECOND JUNGLE BOOK.   Illustrated by J. Lock-
    wood Kipling.   London : Macmillan & Co., and New
    York.   1895.   12mo.   pp. 238.

39. OUT OF INDIA : Things I Saw and Failed to See in Cer-
    tain Days and Nights at Jeypoore and Elsewhere.   New
    York : G. W. Dillingham.   1895.   12mo.   pp. vi–
    346.   (Suppressed.)

40. SOLDIER TALES.   London : Macmillan & Co.   1896.
    12mo.   Illustrated.

41. THE SEVEN SEAS.   London : Methuen & Co.   1896.
    Small 8vo.   Thirty copies on Japan paper and 150 on
    hand-made paper.

42. "CAPTAINS COURAGEOUS " : A Story of the Grand
    Banks.   Illustrations.   New York : The Century Com-
    pany.   1897.   12mo.   pp. viii–323.   Also London :
    Macmillan & Co.

43. STEVE BROWN'S BUNYIP, AND OTHER STORIES. By
    J. A. Barry. Fifth edition. London, 1897. Mac-
    queen. 8vo. Introductory verses by Kipling.

44. AN ALPHABET OF TWELVE SPORTS. First edition.
    London, 1897. William Heinemann. 4to. Illus-
    trated by William Nicholson.

45. THE WRITINGS IN PROSE AND VERSE OF RUDYARD
    KIPLING. *Outward Bound* Edition. 12 volumes.
    8vo. New York : Charles Scribner's Sons. 1897. I.
    "Plain Tales from the Hills." II. "Soldiers Three,
    and Military Tales," Part I. III. "Soldiers Three,
    and Military Tales," Part II. IV. "In Black and
    White." V. "The Phantom 'Rickshaw, and Other
    Stories." VI. "Under the Deodars, and other Sto-
    ries." VII. "The Jungle Book." VIII. "The
    Second Jungle Book." IX. "The Light that Failed."
    X. "The Naulahka." XI. "Verses." XII. "Cap-
    tains Courageous."

46. THE DAY'S WORK. Illustrations. New York : Double-
    day & McClure. 1898. Crown 8vo. pp. 431.

47. A FLEET IN BEING : Notes of Two Trips with the
    Channel Squadron. London : Macmillan & Co.
    1898. Crown 8vo. (A series of articles first contrib-
    uted to the *Morning Post*.)

48. RUDYARD KIPLING'S WORKS. Brushwood Edition.
    15 volumes, including general index. Large 12mo.
    New York : G. P. Putnam's Sons and E. P. Dutton &
    Co., 1899. (This edition includes "The Day's Work,"
    and "Departmental Ditties," and the following stories
    not included in the *Outward Bound* Edition : "Brug-
    glesmith," "Lang Men o' Larut," "Wreck of the
    Visigoth," "Record of Badalia Herodsfoot," and
    "Dream of Duncan Parenness.")

49. FROM SEA TO SEA. Letters of Travel. Includes, besides hitherto unpublished matter, an accurate text of "American Notes," "Letters of Marque," "The City of Dreadful Night," "The Smith Administration," etc. Authorized Edition. New York : Doubleday & McClure. 1899. 2 vols. 12mo. pp. xiii–460 ; ix–400.

50. THE WORKS OF RUDYARD KIPLING. Swastika Edition. Authorized and copyrighted by the author, with a Biographical Sketch by Charles Eliot Norton. Includes, besides the books in the *Outward Bound* Edition, "The Day's Work," "Departmental Ditties," and "From Sea to Sea." 15 vols. 12mo. New York. 1899. (Issued jointly by D. Appleton & Co., the Century Co., and the Doubleday & McClure Co., and marketed by the book department of the H. B. Claflin Co.)

NOTE. — The foregoing list of first editions is intended more for the general reader than for the bibliographer. It is based on the bibliographies of R. F. Roden (*N.Y. Times*) and E. D. North (*Book Buyer.*) The former list has the advantage of embodying annotations added to the earlier bibliography (Mr. North's) by Mr. Kipling.

A BIBLIOGRAPHY OF REFERENCE ARTICLES

Rudyard Kipling. Francis Adams. *Fortnightly Review*, Vol. 56 (o.s.), p. 686, November, 1891.

Mr. Rudyard Kipling's Tales. *Quarterly Review*, Vol. 175, p. 132, July, 1892.

Mr. Kipling's Work, So Far. W. H. Bishop. *Forum*, Vol. 19, p. 476, June, 1895.

Rudyard Kipling as a Poet. Montgomery Schuyler. *Forum*, Vol. 22, p. 406, December, 1896.

The Tales of Rudyard Kipling. *Edinburgh Review*, Vol. 174, p. 132, July, 1891.

Mr. Kipling's Stories. J. M. Barrie. *Contemporary Review*, Vol. 59, p. 364, March, 1891.

Kipling's " Seven Seas " an Atavism. Charlotte Porter. *Poet-Lore*, Vol. 9, No. 2, p. 291, April, 1897.

The Sincerest Form of Flattery. 1. Of Mr. Rudyard Kipling. *Cornhill Magazine*, Vol. 62 (Vol. 15 n.s.), p. 367, October, 1890.

Mr. Rudyard Kipling's Verse. Francis Adams. *Fortnightly Review*, Vol. 60 (o.s.), p. 590, November, 1893.

Cervantes, Zola, Kipling & Co. Brander Matthews. *Cosmopolitan*, Vol. 14, p. 609, March, 1893.

Editor's Study. *Harper's*, Vol. 81, p. 801, October, 1890.

The New Cæsar. Julian Hawthorne. *Lippincott's*, Vol. 46, p. 571, October, 1890.

The Scientific Spirit in Kipling's Work. *Popular Science Monthly*, Vol. 52, p. 269, December, 1897.

The Ascendency of Kipling. *Arena* (editorial), Vol. 19, p. 424, March, 1898.

The Works of Mr. Rudyard Kipling. *Edinburgh Review*, Vol. 187, No. 1 (whole number 383), p. 203, January, 1898.

Kipling's Women. A. B. Maurice. *Bookman* (N.Y.), Vol. 8, No. 5, January, 1899.

The Religion of Mr. Kipling. W. B. Parker. *New World*, December, 1898.

The Religious Element in Kipling's Work. W. B. Parker, *Public Opinion* (N.Y.), Vol. 23, p. 435, Sept. 30, 1897. (Quoted from Boston *Transcript*.)

The Old Saloon. *Blackwood's Magazine*, Vol. 150, p. 728. (Includes a review of "Life's Handicap.")

A Sketch of Rudyard Kipling. Charles D. Lanier. (American) *Review of Reviews*, Vol. 15, p. 173, February, 1897.

The Books of Rudyard Kipling. Goring Cope. *Gentleman's Magazine*, Vol. 273, p. 136, August, 1892.

The Madness of Mr. Kipling. By an Admirer. *Macmillan's Magazine*, No. 470, December, 1898.

Kipling's Tales. *Nation*, Vol. 51, p. 465, Dec. 11, 1890.

Rudyard Kipling the Poet. *London Quarterly Review*, No. 178 (n.s.), No. 58, January, 1898.

Rudyard Kipling and His Stories. *Book Buyer*, Vol. 7, No. 9 (n.s.), October, 1890.

On Some Tales of Mr. Kipling's. S. R. Crockett. *Bookman* (N.Y.), Vol. 1, No. 1, February, 1895.

Rudyard Kipling. John D. Adams. *Book Buyer*, Vol. 13, No. 10, November, 1896.

A Bibliography of First Editions of Rudyard Kipling. Ernest Dressel North. *Book Buyer*, Vol. 13, No. 10, November, 1896.

Mr. Kipling's Ballads of " The Seven Seas." Edmund Clarence Stedman, *Book Buyer*, Vol. 13, No. 10, November, 1896.

Mr. Kipling's Expression of Simple Human Qualities. William Morrow. *Harvard Monthly*, Vol. 26, No. 4, June, 1898.

Mr. Kipling's View of Life. William Morrow. *Harvard Monthly*, Vol. 26, No. 5, July, 1898.

Impressions of Mr. Kipling. H. McCulloch, Jr. *Harvard Monthly*, Vol. 11, No. 4, January, 1891.

Some Minor Poets. *Quarterly Review*, Vol. 186, p. 323, October, 1897. (Seven pages devoted to Kipling.)

Rudyard Kipling's "Seven Seas, and Other Poems." *Review of Reviews* (English), Vol. 14, p. 553, December, 1896.

My First Book. Rudyard Kipling. *McClure's Magazine*, Vol. 3, No. 6, November, 1894.

A French Criticism of Rudyard Kipling. *Review of Reviews* (English), Vol. 5, p. 469, May, 1892. [An abstract of M. W. Bentzon's article in the *Revue des Deux Mondes* for April 1, 1892.]

Recent Poetry. *Nation*, Vol. 63, p. 441, Dec. 10, 1896. ["Seven Seas," etc.]

Kipling in India. E. Kay Robinson. *McClure's Magazine*, Vol. 7, No. 2, July, 1896.

The Laureate of the Larger England. W. D. Howells. *McClure's Magazine*, Vol. 8, No. 5, March, 1897.

The Seven Seas. *Critic*, Vol. 26, New Series, p. 337, Nov. 28, 1896.

"Captains Courageous." *Critic*, Vol. 28, New Series, p. 264, Nov. 6, 1897.

A Gentile Criticism. W. B. Smith. *Critic*, Vol. 29, (n.s.), p. 12, Jan. 1, 1898. [An adverse opinion on the "Recessional." Replied to by T. F. Watson in *Critic* for Jan. 29, 1898.]

Another Jungle Book. Joel Chandler Harris. *Book Buyer*, Vol. 12, No. 11, December, 1895.

A Boy "Who Found Himself." Nathan Haskell Dole. *Book Buyer*, Vol. 15, No. 4, November, 1897. ["Captains Courageous."]

Mr. Kipling's Green Mountain Home. *Critic*, Jan. 21, 1893.

Mr. Kipling's Tales. *Athenæum*, 1890, II., p. 887, December 27.

In Black and White. *Athenæum*, 1890, II., p. 349, September 13.

The Light that Failed. *Athenæum*, 1891, I., p. 497, April 18.

Life's Handicap. *Athenæum*, 1891, II., p. 279, August 29.

Barrack-Room Ballads. *Athenæum*, 1892, I., p. 629, May 14.

The Naulahka. *Athenæum*, 1892, II., p. 154, July 30.

Many Inventions. *Athenæum*, 1893, II., p. 55, July 8.

Departmental Ditties and Soldiers Three. *Athenæum*, 1890, I., p. 527, April 26.

The Jungle Book. *Athenæum*, 1894, I., p. 766, June 16.

The Second Jungle Book. *Athenæum*, 1896, I., p. 278, February 29.

"Captains Courageous." *Athenæum*, 1897, II., p. 589.

The Day's Work. *Athenæum*, 1898, II., p. 521, Oct. 15.

Two Volumes of Satirical Verse. *Spectator*, Vol. 65, p. 345, Sept. 13, 1890.

Rudyard Kipling's First Novel. *Spectator*, Vol. 66, p. 174, Jan. 31, 1891.

Stories by Mr. Rudyard Kipling. *Spectator*, Vol. 67, p. 417, Sept. 26, 1891.

Mr. Kipling on Village Life in America. *Spectator*, Vol. 68, p. 522, April 16, 1892.

Mr. Rudyard Kipling's Ballads. *Spectator*, Vol. 68, p. 644, May 7, 1892.

A Story of West and East. ["Naulahka."] *Spectator*, Vol. 69, p. 196, Aug. 6, 1892.

Soldiers Three. *Spectator*, Vol. 62, p. 403, March 23, 1889.

Mr. Rudyard Kipling's Last Volume. ["Many Inventions."] *Spectator*, Vol. 71, p. 86, July 15, 1893.

Mr. Rudyard Kipling's New Ballads. *Spectator*, Vol. 77, p. 728, Nov. 21, 1896.

Mr. Kipling's Hymn. [A page editorial on the "Recessional."] *Spectator*, Vol. 79, p. 106, July 24, 1897.

"Captains Courageous." *Spectator*, Vol. 79, p. 646, Nov. 6, 1897.

Rudyard Kipling's New Book. ["Day's Work."] *Spectator*, Vol. 81, p. 526, Oct. 15, 1898.

Departmental Ditties. W. M. Hunter. *Academy*, Vol. 34, p. 128, Sept. 1, 1888.

The Light that Failed. Lionel Johnson. *Academy*, Vol. 39, p. 319, April 4, 1891.

Life's Handicap. Lionel Johnson. *Academy*, Vol. 40, p. 327, Oct. 17, 1891.

Barrack-Room Ballads. Lionel Johnson. *Academy*, Vol. 41, p. 509, May 28, 1892.

The Naulahka. Percy Addleshaw. *Academy*, Vol. 42, p. 44, July 16, 1892.

Many Inventions. Percy Addleshaw. *Academy*, Vol. 44, p. 7, July 1, 1893.

The Jungle Book. Percy Addleshaw. *Academy*, Vol. 45, p. 530, June 30, 1894.

The Seven Seas. *Academy*, Vol. 50, p. 377, Nov. 14, 1896.

Mr. Kipling's Seacraft. By a Sailor. *Academy*, Vol. 50, p. 378, Nov. 14, 1896.

Mr. Kipling as Journalist. By one of his Editors. (E. K. R.) *Academy*, Vol. 50, p. 458, Nov. 28, 1896.

Mr. Kipling's Beginnings. *Academy*, Vol. 51, p. 476, May 1, 1897.

The New Kipling. [Review of "Captains Courageous."] *Academy*, Vol. 52, Fiction Supplement, p. 98, Oct. 30, 1897.

Book Reviews Reviewed. ["Captains Courageous."] *Academy*, Vol. 52, p. 359, Oct. 30, 1897.

The Day's Work. *Academy*, Vol. 55, p. 76, Oct. 15, 1898. (Also p. 91 for summary of contemporary opinion on "D.W.")

Mr. Rudyard Kipling. [*The National Observer.*] Quoted in *Critic* (n.s.), Vol. 16, p. 340, Dec. 12, 1891.

Mr. Kipling's Ballads. *Saturday Review*, Vol. 73, p. 580, May 14, 1892.

The Naulahka. *Saturday Review*, Vol. 74, p. 226, Aug. 20, 1892.

Many Inventions. *Saturday Review*, Vol. 75, p. 659, June 17, 1893.

The Seven Seas. *Saturday Review*, Vol. 82, p. 549, Nov. 21, 1896.

Critical Introduction to "Mine Own People." (United States Book Company.) Henry James.

Critical Introduction to "The Courting of Dinah Shadd, and Other Stories." (*Harper's.*) Andrew Lang.

The Secret of the East. [Review of Kipling's Works.] Edward E. Hale, Jr. *Dial* (Chicago), Vol. 23, p. 42, July 16, 1897.

Kipling's Men. Arthur Bartlett Maurice. *Bookman* (N.Y.), Vol. 8, No. 4, December, 1898.

Mr. Kipling at the Cross-Roads. Harry Thurston Peck. *Bookman* (N.Y.), Vol. 8, No. 4, December, 1898.

The Seven Seas. *Bookman* (N.Y.), Vol. 4, No. 5, January, 1897.

The Poetry of Rudyard Kipling. Charles Eliot Norton. *Atlantic Monthly*, Vol, 79, p. 111, January, 1897.

Mr. Kipling's " Captains Courageous." (In " Notable Recent Novels.") *Atlantic Monthly*, Vol. 80, p. 855, December, 1897.

R. Kipling : Comparative Psychologist. (In " Contributors' Club.") *Atlantic Monthly*, Vol. 81, p. 858, June, 1898.

Truth to Fact in " Captains Courageous." *McClure's Magazine*, Vol. 9, p. 618, May, 1897.

Kipling's View of Americans. George Harley McKnight. *Bookman* (N.Y.), Vol. 7, No. 2, April, 1898.

Rudyard Kipling as a Poet. Frank Gaylord Gilman. *Arena*, Vol. 20, No. 3, Sept., 1898.

The Second Jungle Book. *Critic*, Vol. 24 (n.s.), p. 338, Nov. 23, 1895.

Kipling. Robert Bridges. ("Droch.") *Outlook* (N Y.), Vol. 61, No. 5, Feb. 4, 1899.

The Works of Mr. Kipling. *Blackwoods Magazine*, Vol. 164, p. 470, Oct., 1898.

Kipling's Retrocessional. [An editorial on " The Truce of the Bear."] *Nation*, Vol. 67, p. 292, Oct. 20, 1898.

My Contemporaries in Fiction. V. Rudyard Kipling. David Christie Murray. *Canadian Magazine*, Vol. 8, p. 475, April, 1897.

The New Poet of the English Race. J. O. Miller. *Canadian Magazine*, Vol. 8, p. 456, March, 1897.

Mr. Kipling as a Moralist. J. B. P. *Critic*, Vol. 33 (o.s.), p. 360, Nov., 1898.

Mr. Kipling as an Artist. J. B. P. *Critic*, Vol. 33 (o.s.), p. 473, Dec., 1898.

Mr. Kipling on Newfoundland. *Critic*, Vol. 28 (n.s.), p. 236, Oct. 23, 1897.

Stevenson, Kipling, and Anglo-Saxon Imperialism. E. H. Mullin. *Book-Buyer*, Vol. 18, No. 2, March, 1899.

Kipling's Verse-People. Arthur Bartlett Maurice. *Bookman* (N.Y.), Vol. 9, No. 1, March, 1899.

Kipling's Suppressed Works. Luther S. Livingston. *Bookman* (N.Y.), Vol. 9, No. 1, March, 1899.

Kipling's Brattleboro' Home. Dr. Theodore F. Wolfe. *Literary Haunts and Homes*. J. B. Lippincott Co., Philadelphia, 1899, pp. 206-214.

Rudyard Kipling. *Personal Sketches of Recent Authors*. H. T. Griswold (McClurg), 1899.

Kipling's Worth to the World. Julian Hawthorne. *The New Voice*, Vol. 16, No. 11, March 18, 1899.

Kipling at School. Michael Gifford White (an old schoolfellow). *Independent*, Vol. 51, p. 752, March 16, 1899.

Rudyard Kipling in his Vermont Home. The Rev. Charles O. Day. *Congregationalist*, Vol. 84, No. 11, March 16, 1899.

Kipling in America. (American) *Review of Reviews*, Vol. 19, No. 4, April, 1899.

The Boyhood of Famous Authors. William H. Rideing. T. Y. Crowell & Co., 1897, 8vo. Rudyard Kipling, pp. 200-211.

An Apocalypse of Kipling. Prof. George F. Genung, D.D. *Independent*, Vol. 51, p. 888, March 30, 1899. [A study of the poem addressed to Wolcott Balestier, which introduces " Ballads and Barrack-Room Ballads."]

The New Poetry. Maurice Thompson. *Independent*, Vol. 51, p. 608, March 2, 1899. [A conservative estimate of Kipling.]

The Kipling Hysteria. Henry Austin. *Dial*, Vol. 26, p. 327, May 16, 1899. (An adverse criticism.)

Mr. Kipling's "Cynical Jingoism " toward the Brown Man. Henry Wysham Lanier. *Dial*, Vol. 26, p. 389, June 16, 1899.

A Japanese View of Kipling. Adachi Kinnosuke. *Arena*, Vol. 21, No. 6, June, 1899.

Rudyard Kipling and Racial Instinct. Henry Rutgers Marshall. *Century*, Vol. 58, No. 3, July, 1899.

The Religion of Rudyard Kipling. Jabez T. Sunderland. *New England Magazine*, Vol. 20, No. 5, July, 1899.

Rudyard Kipling : A Biographical Sketch. Charles Eliot Norton. *McClure's Magazine*, Vol. 13, No. 3, July, 1899. Republished from the Swastika edition of Kipling's works.

The Unfamiliar Rudyard Kipling. Perriton Maxwell. *Saturday Evening Post*, Philadelphia, Vol. 172, No. 5, July 29, 1899.

INDEX TO AUTHORITIES QUOTED

www.ingramcontent.com/pod-product-compliance
Lightning Source LLC
Chambersburg PA
CBHW030131030726
47498CB00007B/2654